NANCY DREW
girl detective

Real Fake

CAROLYN KEENE

Super Mystery #3

Mystery Behind the Scenes?

I had just dropped off to sleep when something woke me up. There were voices arguing in the hallway.

"Did you get what we needed?" It was a man's low, urgent voice. He sounded familiar.

"While she was interviewing Tyler, I stole her passkey and snuck into her room." It was a woman. She sounded familiar too. "I think I know where we need to break in next."

The voices grew softer. I sat up groggily and strained to listen. I could make out only a few words here and there: "Plan B" and "Diamonds."

Breaking in? Diamonds?

This conversation was definitely getting my attention.

NANCY DREW
girl detective®

Super Mystery

Available from Aladdin Paperbacks

NANCY DREW
girl detective ®

Super Mystery #3

Real Fake

CAROLYN KEENE

Aladdin Paperbacks

New York   London   Toronto   Sydney

❦ ALADDIN PAPERBACKS
An imprint of Simon & Schuster Children's Publishing Division
1230 Avenue of the Americas, New York, NY 10020
Copyright © 2007 by Simon and Schuster, Inc.
All rights reserved, including the right of reproduction in whole or in part in any form.
NANCY DREW, NANCY DREW: GIRL DETECTIVE, ALADDIN PAPER-BACKS, and related logo are registered trademarks of Simon & Schuster, Inc.
The text of this book was set in Bembo.
Manufactured in the United States of America
First Aladdin Paperbacks edition July 2007
10 9 8 7 6 5 4 3 2 1
Library of Congress Control Number 2007921776
ISBN-13: 978-1-4169-3881-1
ISBN-10: 1-4169-3881-8

Contents

A Surprising Invitation

When the phone call came, it wasn't at the most convenient moment. I was in my bedroom, crawling around my hands and knees, searching for an elusive running shoe.

"I know you're here somewhere," I said out loud as I peered under the bed, the desk, the dresser. I loved solving mysteries, but locating missing footwear was not my idea of fun. At least I knew where the left one was; I was wearing it, along with a T-shirt and sweats. It was a beautiful, sunny autumn day, and I was about to go for a run . . . if only I could crack The Case of the Missing Right Shoe.

Just as I was fishing a dust bunny–covered scarf out from under the nightstand, the phone started to ring.

From down the hall, I heard my father call out: "Can you get that, Nancy? I'm on my cell!"

I jumped to my feet, bumping my head on something along the way. "Ow," I muttered under my breath as I picked up the phone. "Hello?" I said, probably a shade abruptly.

"Could I speak to Nancy Drew, please?"

I didn't recognize the fast-talking female voice. "Speaking."

"Hi, Nancy, this is Dee Darby from *Mystery Solved!*"

I did a mental double take. *Mystery Solved!* was one of the most popular reality shows on television. It involved regular people acting like professional detectives and solving made-up mysteries. Each episode took place in a different part of the world. One episode had involved a kidnapped heiress in Hong Kong. Another had featured a rare orchid thief in Brazil.

Dee Darby was the show's creator, executive producer, and host. She *was Mystery Solved!*" Why was she calling *me*?

"Hi, Ms. Darby," I managed after I'd gotten over my total shock.

"I'm sure you know what this is about," Dee Darby said briskly. Before I had a chance to say "Not in the least," she breezed on. "You, Nancy Drew, have been selected to compete in the next episode of *Mystery Solved! Congratulations!*"

My jaw dropped. I felt for the edge of my bed and sat down slowly. I realized that I was still holding the dusty scarf in my hand. I couldn't believe I was going to be a contestant on a reality show!

It had all started six months ago, with an innocent Saturday night of TV watching with my two best friends, George Fayne and Bess Marvin. The three of us had been at George's house, watching the Hong Kong episode and chowing down on a new brand of organic microwave parmesan cheese popcorn that Bess had discovered. When the call for entrants flashed across the TV screen, the two cousins had launched into a full-court press: "Come on, Nancy, you've got to do it!" "You're the best detective in River Heights!" "You're way smarter than that Bucky person who found the missing heiress!" "We dare you!" "We double-dare you!" Et cetera, et cetera.

I had said no about a hundred times, but it hadn't done any good. I finally agreed, just to shut them up. Right then and there, George had logged onto the show's website on one of her many laptops and I had filled out the online entry form, complete with a 250-word essay on why I would be a great *Mystery Solved!* contestant. Among other things, I had mentioned that I'd solved lots of local crimes and cases as an amateur detective-slash-concerned citizen-slash-mystery lover.

It's just for fun, I had told myself. There's no harm in playing along. The chances of getting picked are a zillion to one. . . .

"My assistant producer Elizabeth will overnight the paperwork to you," Dee Darby was saying in her mile-a-minute voice. "Make sure you read the show's rules and regulations handbook with a fine-tooth comb. We'll need the contract back from you within the week, signed and notarized. Oh, and do you have a recent color photo of yourself that you could e-mail to us in jpeg format—say, this afternoon? And before I forget, we have to schedule a time to send a crew to your house. As you know, we like to get footage of the contestants at home. Next Tuesday work for you?

I willed my brain to mobilize. "Next Tuesday," I said, scrambling for a pad of paper and a pen. "Um, I think that's okay. But I'll have to check my calendar and call you back."

"No problem!" Dee Darby exclaimed. "Gotta run, I have to take a meeting. So glad you're on board. We'll talk again soon. Don't hesitate to call if you have any questions."

She rattled off a phone number with a Los Angeles area code as well as an e-mail address where I could send my color photo. Did I *have* a cool-enough photo? I wondered. One that didn't involve me making goofy faces at George and Bess? Or spilling pancake batter all over my lap, like the one our housekeeper, Hannah Gruen, took last Sunday?

Before Dee Darby hung up, I remembered to ask her the most important question of all. "Ms. Darby?" I said quickly. "What's the location for this episode?"

"Brush up on your *français*, Nancy Drew," Dee Darby replied. "You're going to Paris!"

"Did you remember to pack the black miniskirt that I picked out for you at the mall?" Bess asked me for what seemed like the twentieth time.

I craned around to grin at Bess, who was sitting in the backseat of George's car. I was up front with George. The two of them were taking me to the airport for my red-eye to Paris. They had insisted on driving me so I would be on time for my flight. They know me well: Punctuality isn't one of my strong suits.

"Yes, Mom, I packed it," I teased Bess. "And I packed the red top that goes with it too."

"Not red. *Magenta,*" Bess corrected me.

"Okay, magenta," I said. Bess was a fashion freak, to put it mildly. It was one of her lifelong dreams to try to get me to wear something other than my comfy old jeans and the first shirt I grabbed from my closet.

"Let's get our priorities straight here, Cousin,"

George said. She flicked on her right blinker and merged onto the road that led to the airport. "Nancy is going to be solving a mystery. She needs to focus on clues and suspects, not her wardrobe."

"Of course she needs to focus on her wardrobe, George," Bess argued. "She's going to the fashion capital of the world. *And* she's going to be a TV star."

"Don't worry, Bess. I won't embarrass you on national television," I promised.

"Besides, Nancy's under major pressure to win," George went on. "She promised to donate her prize money to River Heights Relief to help build the new homeless shelter, remember? And Mrs. Rackham is matching whatever prize money Nancy brings home. So the stakes are kind of huge."

"Thanks for reminding me, George," I said.

The *Mystery Solved!* grand prize was $100,000. There were eight contestants in all. The contestants could solve the mystery as a team of eight, as miniteams of seven or fewer, or go solo. Allegiances and strategies were constantly changing, so you could start out as part of a team of eight, then split off into a miniteam, then jump ship to another miniteam, then go on your own—and so on and so on. In the end, the prize money was divided among all the winners—or kept by just one winner, as the case may be.

At the airport, George parked the car at the curb. As she retrieved my suitcase from the trunk, she turned to me and said, "Do you have the PDA I gave you?"

"The PD—what?" I asked, puzzled.

"PDA. Personal digital assistant. The one I gave you so we can e-mail each other while you're in Paris," George reminded me patiently.

"Oh, right." I nodded and patted my backpack. "Got it."

George was a computer and electronics expert. She was generously loaning me this high-tech gadget—which she had custom-tailored with my e-mail address—so we could stay in touch across the Atlantic Ocean. There was a strict rule in the *Mystery Solved!* handbook against calling or e-mailing friends or family for help. "I just found this clue in French, Aunt Martha, can you translate it for me?" appeals would not be permitted. There would be periodic spot checks by the crew to enforce this rule. If any contestant broke it, he or she would be asked to leave the show—no exceptions.

Personal calls and e-mails were allowed during downtime, though. The PDA would come in handy for that.

"Don't forget to charge the PDA every night," George said, looking at me meaningfully. She knows that I have a slight, um, problem remembering to charge my cell phone. Apparently, these PDAs required the same care and feeding routine.

"I won't forget," I reassured her.

"And don't forget to carry around extra batteries for the recorder," George added. She was also loaning me her voice-activated microcassette tape recorder. The contestants were allowed to use tape recorders to record witness interviews, personal notes, and so forth. George's was small enough that I could stash it in a jacket pocket.

Bess held up her wrist and tapped on her watch. "Nancy, you've gotta go. It's already after six, and check-in and security can take forever."

I set my suitcase down on the sidewalk and gave Bess and George big hugs. People milled around us, hurrying to their own flights or jockeying for cabs. "I wish you guys could come along and be on my team," I said wistfully. "I always do my best mystery solving with you guys."

"We'll be with you in spirit," George said, hugging me back. "Whenever you hear that voice in your head saying 'Don't trust that suspect,' that'll be me."

"And whenever you hear that voice in your head saying 'Wear the silver necklace with the black dress,' that'll be me," Bess joked.

I laughed. I knew I'd miss the two of them. I was going to have to use George's PDA a *lot*.

I said my final good-byes and headed into the terminal with my backpack and suitcase. I found the check-in counter for my flight and got in line behind several dozen people. Standing there, I wondered what was waiting for me in Paris. What was the mystery going to be? And who were the other seven contestants?

An hour and a half and several lines, security checks, and cups of Darjeeling tea later, I finally took my seat on the plane. I was wedged in between a young guy with dreads and a mother with a baby on her lap. The baby stared at me, his blue eyes huge. I smiled at him and wiggled my fingers hello. His face twisted, and he started to cry.

"Oh, I'm so sorry," I apologized to the mother.

The mother smiled wearily and reached into her bag for a snack. "Oh, please don't worry. He's just hungry and tired."

"Aren't we all," the guy on the other side of me remarked.

Just then, something started beeping in my backpack. What *was* that noise? I wondered. I reached down and tried to find the source.

Shuffling through my backpack, I located a small blue plastic thing. It was George's PDA. The mailbox icon was flashing. My first e-mail! It was probably George doing a test run. Or maybe it was Bess with a last-minute fashion tip.

The baby stopped crying and stretched a jam-covered hand for the PDA. I gently moved it away, which unfortunately made him start crying again. I pressed several buttons, just as George had taught me to do. After a moment, a message flashed across the tiny screen:

GET READY FOR A BUMPY RIDE, NANCY DREW.

I frowned at the screen. Get ready for a bumpy ride? What did that mean? And who had sent it?

Maybe George and Bess are playing a joke, I thought.

I pressed several more buttons to back up to the original screen. The sender was neither one of my friends. It was someone named DOOMSDAY246.

DOOMSDAY246?

Who was this person? How had he or she gotten my e-mail address? I felt a shiver of apprehension.

The plane's engines rumbled to life. "Fasten your seat belts," the pilot announced over the loudspeakers. "Please turn off all cell phones, pagers, laptops, and other portable electronic devices." I quickly switched off the PDA.

Outside the window, dozens of lights twinkled against the night sky as planes began to taxi toward the runway. Who was DOOMSDAY246? I wondered again. And what did his—or her—message mean?

2

The Competition

The limousine glided down a cobblestoned street and turned onto the Boulevard St. Germaine. I blinked as I stared out the window at a row of charming little shops and restaurants. Paris. I couldn't believe I was in Paris!

"We will be at the hotel soon, mademoiselle," the driver said to me in heavily accented English. "If you would like refreshments, please help yourself to sparkling water or juice."

"Thank you. I mean, *merci beaucoup*."

"*De rien*."

We drove by a crowded outdoor café; people were talking, drinking coffee, reading the newspaper. In the distance, I could see the slender top of the Eiffel Tower. My plane had arrived at Paris's Charles de

Gaulle Airport at 11:00 a.m. Paris time, which was 4:00 a.m. my time—seven hours behind. My body ached from fatigue; it had been hard to sleep on the plane, especially wedged between two other passengers and a fussy baby. But I couldn't imagine closing my eyes now, as much as I needed a nap. Being in Paris was electrifying.

The flight had been long, but without incident. I had not experienced a "bumpy ride," despite the strange warning from DOOMSDAY246. The e-mail had probably been a mistake or a prank. Still, I had forwarded it to George from the Paris airport to see if she could shed some light on its sender. She was a computer wiz times fifty. If anyone could solve a cyberpuzzle, it was George.

We eventually reached the Hotel Royale, which was located in the sixth arrondissement. Paris was divided into twenty arrondissements, which were the equivalent of neighborhoods. The Hotel Royale was a large, elegant white building with marble columns and tall windows. Beautiful red flowers spilled over the sides of balcony boxes. Above the entrance, the French flag billowed in the crisp autumn breeze.

As soon as the limousine pulled to a stop, a well-dressed doorman rushed to open my door.

"*Bonjour,* mademoiselle. *Bienvenue,*" he said. Mentally, I translated: "Hello, miss. Welcome." I had spent much of the last few weeks taking an intensive online French course that George had found for me.

"*Merci beaucoup,*" I said, thanking him.

Just then, there was a commotion behind him. I realized that a small crowd was swarming toward me, including a guy with a big video camera hoisted on one shoulder and a woman wearing a trench coat and dark glasses.

"Nancy Drew!" the woman exclaimed. She flashed me a charming smile. "Welcome to Paris! Are you ready to solve a mystery?"

It took me only a second to realize that the woman was Dee Darby. She looked just like she did on TV and in magazines.

Behind her, a photographer pointed his camera at me and started clicking away. I didn't have time to wonder if my hair, which I hadn't combed since I left River Heights, looked good.

I grinned weakly at the photographer and then at Dee Darby. "Hi, Ms. Darby. Thank you for having me on your show."

"We're so glad you're here," Ms. Darby replied. "Is this your first time in the City of Lights? What do you think so far? Do you have a message for your friends and family back home?" The guy with the video camera moved closer to me.

"Hi, Dad. Hi, Hannah. Hi, Bess. Hi, George," I

said, waving at the video camera. I knew that wasn't very original, but I didn't know what else to say.

Ms. Darby's charming smile suddenly disappeared. "Cut the camera, Jean Alain," she said abruptly. The cameraman—a cute young guy with long, curly black hair—obeyed. I gulped, wondering if I had done something wrong.

But apparently it had nothing to do with me. "Elizabeth!" Ms. Darby yelled. "Elizabeth, where are you?"

"Yes, Ms. Darby! I'm here!"

A young woman came rushing up. I had spoken to her on the phone; she was one of the show's assistant producers. She had short red hair and big tortoise-shell glasses. She wobbled precariously on her high-heeled shoes like a newborn colt learning how to walk. There was a big coffee stain across the front of her white blouse.

"Yes, Ms. Darby?" she said breathlessly. She adjusted the load in her arms: a huge pile of files, a couple of fat manila envelopes, a clipboard, and a coffee cup.

Ms. Darby glared at her. "Elizabeth! Where is that script for the new promo? You were supposed to have twenty copies to me an hour ago."

Elizabeth blushed. "They, uh—the hotel's copying machine ran out of ink and the man at the front desk wasn't sure if they had any more ink cartridges, so—"

"Elizabeth," Ms. Darby said in an icy-cold voice.

"I . . . do . . . not . . . want . . . to . . . hear . . . about . . . it. Just get it done. Do you understand? Or do you want to continue broadcasting your incompetence to the entire sixth arrondissement?"

Elizabeth's cheeks grew even redder. "Yes, Ms. Darby," she said in a voice barely above a whisper. She turned and rushed back into the hotel.

I felt sorry for poor Elizabeth. I was also surprised by Ms. Darby's nastiness. There were obviously two sides to the famous TV personality. I reminded myself to be careful around her.

Ms. Darby turned to me. Her charming smile was back on her face. It was like a light switch: on, then off, then on again. "Let's go inside and get you checked in," she said pleasantly. "I think you'll like your room; it's a luxury suite. All the other contestants have already arrived. You'll be meeting them at our 'Meet the Contestants' taping, which is in"—she glanced at her watch—"forty-five. You need to hurry so you can get into hair and makeup." She glanced over her shoulder. "Michaela, we need another sound check in the Savoie Room. Gaston, make sure hotel security keeps the other guests out for the next two . . . no, three hours. Come on, people, let's look alive here!"

With that, Ms. Darby turned and swept through the hotel doors, doormen bowing in her wake. I stood there for a second, trying to take it all in. Everything was happening so fast.

The cameraman named Jean Alain turned to me and winked. "Welcome to . . ." He paused.

"Paris?" I finished.

He shook his head and grinned. "Television."

I laughed, glad for someone with a sense of humor.

The next few weeks were going to be quite an adventure.

Elizabeth took me up to my suite, which was on the sixth floor. It was enormous—probably four times as big as my room at home, I guessed. It was furnished with a king-size bed, a dresser, a small table, a desk, and an entertainment center with a plasma-screen TV, DVD player, and CD system. There was a vase of fresh flowers on the nightstand, with a welcome note from Dee Darby. There was another note with greetings from the hotel management on my pillow, along with a box of chocolates. Needless to say, I was feeling very welcomed.

"Do you need anything?" Elizabeth asked me in a shy, quiet voice. "I mean, you know, if you need a bottle of water or some snacks or a toothbrush or whatever."

I set my luggage on the floor. "I'm fine, thanks," I replied. "So, how long have you been working for *Mystery Solved!*?"

"Oh, I don't know—kind of forever," Elizabeth said. "I'm not sure how I ended up in television, exactly. I majored in art in college. I thought I wanted to be a painter or something. But being a painter doesn't exactly pay the bills." She smiled awkwardly.

"Ms. Darby seems like a, um, tough boss," I said sympathetically.

Elizabeth sighed. "Oh, well, yeah. It was definitely hard the first couple of months. But now I'm kind of used to the Boss Lady." She lowered her voice and added, "Plus, I've found little ways to get back at her. Like, sometimes, I'll hide her reading glasses so she can't find them. Or I'll mix up her notes when she's not looking so that the page numbers are all wrong. It drives her crazy." She giggled.

"Wow," I said. I felt sorry for poor Elizabeth.

A panicked expression crossed Elizabeth's face. "Oh! I shouldn't be telling you these things, should I? Please don't say anything to the Boss Lady or anyone else, okay? I'll totally get fired. Please, Nancy?"

"Your secret's safe with me," I assured her.

Elizabeth let out a deep breath. "Oh, whew. Thank you so much!" She reached into her pocket and pulled out a business card and a pen. She scribbled some numbers onto it. "Listen, if you need anything, just call me, okay? This is my private cell, plus I wrote down my room number here at the hotel."

I took the card from her. "Thanks. That's really sweet of you. I'm sure I'll be okay, though."

Elizabeth gave me a funny look. "That's what all the contestants think, in the beginning. But they change their minds pretty fast. While you're on this show, Nancy, you're going to need all the friends you can get."

The Savoie Room was one of the private conference rooms at the Hotel Royale. It had gold-gilded antique furniture and ornate murals on the walls, which someone explained were trompe l'oeil: "to trick the eye." The name came from the fact that the murals were supposed to fool you. Like the mural of the window with a pretty landscape outside; it was so realistic it almost made you think you were looking through a real window at a real country scene, instead of a painting.

It was hard to feel like you were in a three-hundred-year-old room surrounded by three-hundred-year-old murals and antiques, though, because the place was jammed with modern production equipment: lights, cameras, booms, microphones, you name it. We were taping the "Meet the Contestants" segment. I remembered this segment from the *Mystery Solved!* episodes I had watched.

The seven other contestants and I were sitting in a row of chairs, facing Ms. Darby and the cameras. I

19

was at one end of the row. I glanced to my left and tried to check everyone out, discreetly. My competition consisted of four men and three other women. I wondered which of them would end up being my allies—or enemies—or both.

"We'll be starting in just a second, everyone," Ms. Darby announced.

I sat back in my seat and touched my hair, which was stiff with hairspray. A girl named Anaïs had styled it and done my makeup. She had explained to me that TV makeup was way heavier than regular, every-day makeup. She wasn't kidding. My face was caked with beige foundation; my cheeks were covered with pink blush; my eyes were outlined with blue eye shadow, brown eye liner, and brown mascara; and my lips were layered with lip gloss, lipstick, and lip liner. Even Bess, who worshiped makeup as much as she worshiped fashion, would probably freak out if she saw me now.

"Okay, we're ready to roll," Ms. Darby said. Big, bright lights clicked on, and the video cameras swarmed in on us. I took a deep breath. It was happening!

Ms. Darby switched on her charming TV smile. "I want to know about each and every one of you," she said. "Who are you? Why are you here? Hamish Watson, let's start with you."

20

The cameras zoomed to a guy at the other end of the row. He had dark brown hair and a thick mustache. He was dressed in a gray suit with a matching vest, cape, and hat. His outfit looked old-fashioned and out of place somehow, as though it were from another century.

"Hi, everyone, I'm Hamish," the guy said with a nervous smile. "I, uh, own a mystery bookstore in Vermont. It's called Books to Die For, ha-ha. I'm also the president of our local Sherlock Holmes Society. My mother was the president before me. My parents named me John Hamish—after Dr. John Hamish Watson of course."

That's it, I thought. He's dressed like he's out of a Sherlock Holmes mystery.

"Who's Dr. John Hamish Watson?" a young woman next to him piped up.

Hamish stared at her. His expression said, *you're kidding, right?* "Uh, that would be Dr. John Hamish Watson as in Dr. Watson, Sherlock Holmes's right-hand man," he explained. "Arthur Conan Doyle created the two characters for his mystery stories. Sherlock Holmes is probably the most famous fictional detective in all of history."

"Thanks so much, Hamish," Ms. Darby said.

I thought for a moment about the *Mystery Solved!* episodes I had seen. The "Meet the Contestants" segment never showed Ms. Darby; it just showed the contestants, talking about themselves like Hamish had just done. The only time Ms. Darby appeared in the segment was when she gave her big "Welcome to *Mystery Solved!*" speech. I realized that the footage that was being taped now would be edited later on, cutting out most of the parts with Ms. Darby talking and probably other parts as well.

It was really interesting being behind the scenes and seeing how a reality TV show was made. It was like being in a play—the rehearsals, the making of the sets, and so forth, and then watching it all come together on opening night. Except in this case, "opening night" would be after I'd returned home to River Heights and was watching along with the rest of America as the Paris episode aired on television.

Ms. Darby turned to the woman who had asked about Dr. Watson. The woman was tall and attractive, with long, wavy auburn hair, large brown eyes, and a deep tan. "Wendy Garcia, let's go to you next. Who are you and why are you here?"

"Hey, everyone, I'm Wendy," the woman said, tossing her hair over her shoulders. "I'm from Miami. I'm an actress. I do some modeling, too. I'm here because I'm a huge mystery fan. And *Mystery Solved!*? It's like my favorite TV show, ever."

"Have you done any TV before, Wendy?" Ms. Darby asked her.

Wendy studied her perfectly manicured nails. Not that I'm an expert, but they looked way too long for doing any serious detective work. One round of digging for buried clues or searching for a hidden wall panel, and they'd be history. "Sure," Wendy replied. "I did a Quik Relief cough syrup commercial last year. I was the girl in the back, coughing."

Ms. Darby raised an eyebrow. "That's terrific, Wendy. And what about you, Chen Li? What's your story?"

Chen had short, spiky black hair and was sporting a black T-shirt that said LAN PARTY. What on earth was a LAN party? I wondered.

"Right," Chen said in a quiet voice. "I'm from L.A., and I design video games. My specialty is mystery video games."

"Well, that is just too cool, Chen," Ms. Darby told him. "Althea Eisner, let's hear from you next."

Althea was a willowy woman with light brown hair tied back in a ponytail. She wore lots of silver and turquoise jewelry. "Hey, everyone. I'm from Albuquerque, New Mexico."

"And what do you do in Albuquerque, Althea?" Ms. Darby prompted her.

"I'm a history and literature double major at the university," Althea replied. "I've been reading mysteries since I was in kindergarten. It's kind of an obsession of mine."

"Sounds like we have a serious mystery buff on our hands," Ms. Darby remarked. "Tyler Cox, what about you?"

"Tyler J. Cox," the guy sitting next to Mary said in a no-nonsense, all-business voice. He was dressed in an expensive-looking navy blue suit with a white shirt with gold cufflinks. He was bald and tan, with chiseled features. "I'm from New York City. I'm an investment banker. Love mysteries. Love the show. Oh, and by the way, I plan to win."

"You sound very confident, Tyler," Ms. Darby said. "How about you, Mary Lee Abernathy? What's your story?"

Mary Lee sat up and beamed. She was petite, with supercurly blond hair, big blue eyes, and dimples. She wore a lacy pink dress that made me think of fancy afternoon tea parties.

"Hey, y'all," Mary Lee said with a thick Southern accent. "I'm from Mississippi. I am such a fan of *Mystery Solved!*, and I can't tell you how tickled I am to be here! Really, it is such an honor! When Ms. Darby called me at home to tell me the good news, I screamed so loud that my neighbor thought there was a burglar in my house."

"Yes, I do remember that scream." Ms. Darby covered her ears and made a funny face. Everyone laughed. "Thanks for that story, Mary Lee. Let's go to

Fish next. By the way, Fish, do you have a last name?"

Fish had sun-bleached blond hair, green eyes, and a big, easy smile. He wore a tie-dyed T-shirt and a pair of faded denim cutoffs. "Nah, I'm just Fish," he said in a friendly voice.

"Tell us about yourself, Fish," Ms. Darby said.

Fish leaned back in his chair. "Well, first of all, I just want to say that Paris seems way cool. The only problem with it is that it's not on the ocean. Other than that, it's pretty excellent."

"You're from Hawaii, right?" Ms. Darby asked him. "What's your connection to mysteries?"

Fish's expression became serious. "Life is a mystery, Ms. Darby. The universe is a mystery. And the biggest mystery of all is the ocean. You ask yourself: Where does that wave come from? Where does it go? What am I, a mere surfer-slash-truth-seeker, compared to the great ebb and flow of the tides?"

"Ladies and gentlemen, I think we have a philosopher among us," Ms. Darby said.

And then she turned to face me. "And last but not least, Nancy Drew," she said.

My heart skipped a beat. I was up!

"I'm from a town called River Heights," I began. "I guess you could call me an amateur detective. I've been solving mysteries in my hometown and in other places, too, since I was in elementary school.

Our local police chief uses me to help him solve cases sometimes."

"Well, sounds like we have another serious mystery lover on our hands," Ms. Darby quipped. She stood up and began walking around the room. The cameras followed her every move. "Hamish. Wendy. Chen. Althea. Tyler. Mary Lee. Fish. Nancy. Welcome to *Mystery Solved!* Very soon, the eight of you will hear all about the mystery you are to solve. Very soon, the eight of you will start investigating clues and interviewing suspects. Very soon, the eight of you will decide to join forces or go your separate ways, knowing that you can change your mind at any turn. Very soon, you will begin your journey toward international fame and glory and a hundred-thousand-dollar grand prize as you become . . . *Mystery Solved!* detectives!"

This was the same welcome speech she always gave on the show, so I had heard it before. Still, I felt goose bumps. This is not reality, I reminded myself. This is just reality television. Even so, I was psyched. I had never met a mystery I couldn't solve, and I couldn't wait to start tackling this one.

3

A Parisian Puzzle

MILLION-DOLLAR NECKLACE STOLEN AT DIPLOMAT'S PARTY
Police Stumped

(Paris, France.) During a lavish birthday party thrown by Gillian Gory for her husband, British diplomat Sir Adrian Gory, a thief or thieves made off with Mrs. Gory's prized diamond necklace.

Odile Olivier, one of the Gorys' maids, told the police that the necklace is from Laurier Jewelers, the internationally renowned jewelry store. Reputed to be worth over $1 million U.S., the necklace was taken from the Gorys' safe at their townhouse on Rue de Grenelle just as the party was getting started.

"It all happened so quickly," Olivier said. "All of us were terribly upset. No one more so than Sir Adrian and Madame Gillian of course."

Guests included over a hundred friends, family members, and prominent local citizens, according to a guest list provided by one of the Gorys' staff. Right now, the police have no suspects.

"Anyone who can solve this mystery will be generously rewarded," said Sir Adrian, whose 61st birthday was the occasion for the celebration. "You could say that this theft is truly an Enigma."

I glanced up from the *International Post* article. It was Monday morning, and the seven other contestants and I were sitting around a large round table in the Savoie Room. Dee Darby, Elizabeth, and other crew members were there as well. The cameras were rolling.

Ms. Darby had just presented us with a black folder marked DOSSIER: PRIVATE AND CONFIDENTIAL. The dossier had contained the *International Post* article—which wasn't a real article, just a prop for the show—and a color photograph of a stunning diamond necklace from Laurier Jewelers. I had been to the Laurier store in New York City once, on a vacation with my father. It was the fanciest store I had ever been in; Dad had joked that it would probably cost him a year's salary just to buy one of their simple silver key chains engraved with the famous *L* logo.

So this was the mystery we were to solve: a missing diamond necklace from a world-famous jeweler. Already my brain was churning over angles, suspects, possibilities.

"Contestants, now that you've read your dossiers, let me explain a few very important things," Ms. Darby said. "First, each and every one of you will have to decide on teams. Do you want to work as a team of eight, as miniteams of fewer than eight, or on your own? You have to make that decision now, this morning, although you can change your mind whenever and as often you want. Remember that, in the end, if you win as part of a team or miniteam, the hundred-thousand-dollar grand prize will be split equally."

She went on. "Next: Since you are detectives working on a mystery, you will have free reign to spend your days and nights conducting your investigations. There will be no preset schedule. Go wherever your clues and so forth take you."

She added, "There are, however, two exceptions to the 'no preset schedule' rule. First, you will be downstairs at 7:30 a.m. each morning for hair and makeup. Then, at 8:00 a.m., we will all gather in this room. I'll tell you more about that in a minute. Second, I will grab each of you daily for individual interviews. Those are called the 'Candid Confessions' segments. Participation in those segments is not voluntary; it's mandatory."

I nodded to myself. I remembered those "Candid Confessions" segments from the other episodes. You never saw Ms. Darby during those segments; she was the "invisible interviewer," like she was 90 percent of the time. But I had the distinct impression that as the interviewer, she tried to get the contestants to bad-mouth each other, talk about their "real feelings" about being on the show, and so forth. I wasn't looking forward to those interviews. I made a mental note to be extra-careful about what I said.

"And, contestants? Just a reminder that you will be followed at all times by one or more cameramen," Ms. Darby continued. "You will never *not* be on camera, except when you are in your hotel rooms after hours."

Fish raised his hand. "Do we get to go to the bathroom without the cameras?"

"Yes, of course," Ms. Darby replied. "Reality TV isn't *that* real." Everyone laughed.

Ms. Darby stood up. "And now I want to introduce you to someone very special," she announced.

The door to the Savoie Room opened and a man strolled in. The cameras swung toward him. The man appeared to be in his midthirties. He was tall and handsome, with longish blond hair that brushed his collar. He wore an elegant navy blue suit and purple tie. Something about him said: *really, really rich.*

Ms. Darby and the man kissed each other on both cheeks. I noticed that this was how people often greeted each other in Paris, instead of handshakes or hugs or one-cheek kisses.

"Contestants, this is Leo Laurier," Ms. Darby told us. "He is the president of Laurier Jewelers and son of Maximilian Laurier, who founded the company. Laurier Jewelers has graciously lent us the beautiful diamond necklace for this show. Leo Laurier is here to tell us about it."

"*Bonjour*, everyone," Mr. Laurier said. His English was perfect, and graced with a hint of a French accent. "Welcome to Paris. As Madame Darby said, we at Laurier Jewelers are proud to have our signature diamond necklace, known as the Contessa, be a part of *Mystery Solved!* Unlike other TV shows that might use a *fake* diamond necklace, *Mystery Solved!* wanted to be completely authentic. Laurier Jewelers was happy to help out. The missing necklace you will be searching for is one hundred percent real. It is worth over a million dollars."

I frowned. I was surprised to hear Mr. Laurier's announcement. I had assumed that the missing diamond necklace would be a prop. It seemed really risky for the show to use a real diamond necklace. What if someone who was *not* involved in the show happened to stumble upon wherever the "thief" was hiding it and steal it—for real?

I shook my head slightly and suppressed a chuckle. This was getting really confusing. I was in a reality TV show where I had to solve a fake mystery about a fake criminal pretending to steal a real necklace—which could in theory get stolen by a real criminal. How mixed up was that?

"In case any of you are wondering about security," Mr. Laurier said, as if reading my mind, "there is a small, almost invisible security device attached to the necklace. If anyone touches it, it will immediately set off a silent alarm and activate a tracking device. Ms. Darby and I are the only ones who possess a remote mechanism that can turn off the security device. Which of course we will do when one of you finds the necklace." He smiled.

"Thank you, Leo Laurier," Ms. Darby said, blowing him air kisses. He waved and left the room.

Ms. Darby turned her attention back to us. "Lovely man. Now. I said I'd tell you more about what we'll be doing each morning at 8:00 a.m. We're going to be doing something a little different this season."

She gestured to Elizabeth, who rushed over and handed her a small blue envelope. Hamish, who was sitting next to me, leaned over. "I wonder what that is?" he whispered.

"No idea," I whispered back. "I've never seen that blue envelope on the show."

"I am introducing a new segment to *Mystery Solved!* called the 'Clue Challenge' segment," Ms. Darby explained. "Inside this blue envelope is a clue to the mystery. Each morning, I will give you all a puzzle to solve. The first one to solve the puzzle wins the clue for the day. Of course, if you are a member of a team or miniteam, you can share clues with one another." She added, "You can also try to trade clues with people you're competing against."

"Sounds cool," Chen spoke up.

"So, what's the first challenge?" Tyler said impatiently.

As if on cue, Elizabeth handed each of us a folded-up sheet of paper. I opened mine. On it was written a single word: TECPUSS.

"I don't get it," Wendy said, peering down at her own slip of paper, looking confused. "*That's* the puzzle?"

"That's the puzzle. The first one who solves it gets

this clue." Ms. Darby held up the small blue envelope and dangled it in the air.

I stared at the word. TECPUSS. Was it some sort of name? A company, a brand, a product? Did the "puss" part of it have something to do with cats?

I pulled a pen out of my pocket and started scribbling. *TEC PUSS. TE C PUSS.*

Then it occurred to me that "TECPUSS" might be an anagram for something. I quickly started rearranging the letters. *TES* . . . no. *CES* . . . no. *PES* . . . that didn't work either. I tried several more possibilities.

And then I hit on something and alarm bells went off in my brain. *SUS. SUSTECP. SUSCEPT. SUSPECT.*

I flung my hand into the air. "I got it!" I practically shouted.

Ms. Darby turned to me. "Yes, Nancy Drew?"

"It's 'suspect,'" I announced.

Tyler threw his pen down on the floor. "I was just about to say that," he said in a tight, irritated voice.

"And we have the first winner of the first 'Clue Challenge,'" Ms. Darby said with a smile. "Nancy Drew, come over and get your prize." She held out the blue envelope.

I stood up and walked over to her. She handed me the envelope. Everyone's eyes were on me as I opened it; the cameras were on me too.

Inside the envelope was a small blue card that matched the envelope. On the card was a single word:

ART

Art, I thought. Okay. The solution to this mystery has something to do with art.

"I want Nancy on my team," Wendy said, raising her hand.

"Yeah, obviously—me, too," Chen added.

"She's on *my* team," Tyler insisted.

Althea, Mary Lee, Fish, and Hamish also chimed in. Being in possession of clue number one, I was suddenly the most popular person in the room.

"This is a good time for you all to make a decision about teams," Ms. Darby said. "Do you want to start Day 1 as a team, as miniteams, or on your own?"

"I don't care, as long as Nancy is on my team," Wendy said.

"Of course, there is an obvious problem with joining forces," Hamish spoke up. "How do we know we can trust one another?"

"We don't, dude," Chen replied.

"You're a real optimist, aren't you, Li?" Althea teased him. He grinned at her.

"Oh, I *so* don't want to work alone," Mary Lee

said, pouting. "I *do* believe two heads are better than one. And three or four or five or six or seven or eight heads are definitely better than one. Don't y'all agree?"

"I'll be your partner, Mary Lee," Fish offered, staring dreamily at her. Uh-oh, someone has a crush, I thought.

"I have a suggestion . . . ," I began, but I was promptly cut off by Tyler.

"Okay, this is the plan," he announced, rising to his feet. "We'll work as a team of eight. We'll operate with a top-down hierarchy so that everyone knows what they're doing and no one is duplicating tasks. That's the most efficient way."

The other contestants exchanged glances.

"Are we all on board?" Tyler demanded. "Well? Come on, people, we don't have all day. Let's see a show of hands."

"Uh, sure," Wendy said, raising her hand.

"I guess so." Mary Lee raised her hand too. One by one, everyone raised their hands, including me.

Tyler nodded, looking pleased. "Okay. Now that we're a team, Nancy, you can share your clue with us. What is it?"

I hesitated for a second. Things were moving so fast. But Tyler was right. We were a team. It made sense for me to share my clue.

"Art," I said. "*A-r-t*. That's what it says." I passed the card around.

Mary Lee peered at the card when it reached her. She turned it sideways, then upside down, then right side up again. "Maybe there's something written on here in invisible ink," she suggested.

"That's a crazy idea," Tyler said dismissively.

Mary Lee pouted. "That is *so* not a nice thing to say."

"Maybe the thief is hiding the necklace in an art museum or gallery," Hamish suggested.

"Or maybe the thief's name is Art–something," Wendy added.

Tyler grabbed the card from Wendy and studied it briefly. "Okay, this clue doesn't make a lot of sense now, but maybe it will later on," he said. "Here's what we're going to do, people. As a first step, we'll all head over to Sir Adrian Gory's townhouse and check out the crime scene. We can question witnesses, get the whole story. We can also comb the place for clues. Come on, let's move it. It's show time!"

He scooped up his dossier and headed for the door. Ms. Darby gestured to one of the cameramen, who scrambled after him.

Althea frowned at Tyler. "Who made *him* boss?" she muttered.

"Guys like him always think they're in charge," Chen said. He didn't sound too happy either.

Still, everyone got up from their seats and followed Tyler. Even if he *was* acting superbossy, his plan made sense. It was logical that the first step in the case would be to go over to the Gorys' townhouse.

I tucked my dossier into my bag and headed for the door along with the others. I also double-checked to make sure that I had George's micro-cassette tape recorder with me. I planned to record all the witness interviews, word for word, so that I wouldn't miss a thing.

As I exited the conference room, I thought about how I would have to navigate this tricky new territory: solving a mystery with other people.

Other people who weren't George or Bess, that is.

"I think the two of us need to stick together," Hamish told me in a low, conspiratorial voice.

Hamish and I were walking with the others down the Rue de Grenelle. We were on our way to the Gorys' townhouse, which was just a few blocks from our hotel. The Rue de Grenelle was a pretty street lined with elegant townhouses, hotels, and cafés. Many locals stopped to stare at us curiously. We must be quite the sight: eight Americans, a huge TV crew, and Dee Darby in her trench coat and dark glasses, barking orders at poor Elizabeth.

I turned and regarded Hamish with a quizzical expression. "Why do you say that?" I asked him. For a second, I stared at his outfit in fascination. He was wearing the same old-fashioned suit, cape, and hat as yesterday. He really did look like a character out of a Sherlock Holmes story.

"It's obvious that we're the only true mystery experts in this motley bunch," Hamish went on. "You have years of experience solving cases. I am the president of my local Sherlock Holmes Society. Enough said."

"I appreciate your confidence," I told him with a smile. "Some of the others seem pretty smart, though. We should wait and see."

While we walked, I snuck a look at the blue PDA, which I was carrying in my coat pocket. I had turned the volume off. There was nothing new from George. She had e-mailed me a few hours ago saying that she would try to track down the identity of DOOMSDAY246.

"We have to protect ourselves, Nancy," Hamish warned. "I sense a lot of potential backstabbers among us. Tyler, for example. I don't trust him one bit. As for Chen and Althea, I saw them whispering in the hotel lobby last night. I think they might be forming a secret alliance. In fact, all this reminds me of one of Sherlock Holmes's most fascinating cases, The Man with the Twisted Lip. . . ."

Hamish sure was paranoid. But he was making me kind of paranoid too. I glanced nervously over my shoulder.

Just then, I noticed two things.

First, I noticed Jean Alain walking about three feet behind us on the sidewalk. His camera was pointed right at Hamish and me. Had he recorded our entire conversation?

Second, I noticed Mary Lee near Jean Alain, a pink notebook in hand. She was scribbling furiously. When she saw me looking at her, she blushed and slapped her notebook shut.

I realized at that moment that nothing I said or did during the next few weeks would be private.

Nothing.

I had to be careful. *Really* careful.

4

Another Clue

I have been in some fancy houses in my life, but Sir Adrian Gory's house was one of the fanciest. The front hallway had a glittering crystal chandelier, a marble staircase leading to an upper floor, and a six-foot-high modern sculpture of an I'm-not-sure-what. The rooms were filled with antiques, fine art, and Oriental rugs. There were vases of long-stemmed roses everywhere, filling the air with their sweet, heady fragrance.

It looked like a rich person's home . . . except that no one actually lived here. The lavish townhouse had been rented—and decorated—just for the *Mystery Solved!* episode. How bizarre was that?

We were all in the living room getting settled in— the contestants, Dee Darby, Elizabeth, and the crew—

when a woman came rushing through the doorway. She was petite and slim, with short silver hair and blue eyes. She was dressed in a long lavender caftan.

It's Sir Adrian's wife, Gillian Gory, I thought immediately. Or rather, it's an actress playing the part of Mrs. Gory. I wasn't sure what we were supposed to say to her. Should we address her as Mrs. Gory, or as her real name, or what?

"Oh, I am so relieved that you detectives are finally here!" the woman cried out, stretching her arms toward us. Jean Alain zoomed his camera in on her. "The police haven't made any headway whatsoever. You must find my diamond necklace. You must!" She clasped her hands to her chest and looked as though she was about to faint.

Okay, that answered *that* question. She was in character as Mrs. Gory. We were obviously supposed to go along with that.

A small silver poodle—the same color as Mrs. Gory's hair—came running after her, barking excitedly. It had a lavender collar around its neck, studded with shiny rhinestones. Across the room, I noticed a white, orange, and black calico cat cleaning its whiskers and pretending not to notice the dog. The Gory "family" had "pets"! The show was definitely into authenticity.

"Contestants, meet Mrs. Gillian Gory," Ms. Darby

said, stepping forward. The poodle barked sharply. "And this is, uh, Mrs. Gory's dog—"

"Pomme Frite," Mrs. Gory said. "It means 'french fry.' Doesn't it, you darling Boo-Boo, you?" She patted the poodle on its head.

We went through a round of introductions. Just as Hamish started telling Mrs. Gory about how he was named after Dr. Watson, a tall, broad-shouldered man entered the living room. He was dressed in an elegant-looking gray suit and black bow tie that complemented his grayish black hair and beard.

"What's all this?" the man said in a booming voice. He had the same thick British accent as his wife. "Gil, who are these people?" he added, glancing at Mrs. Gory.

"Adrian, dear, these are the detectives," Mrs. Gory replied, hooking her arm through his. "They're here to help us find my necklace. Please be polite to them," she added in a whisper.

Sir Adrian stared at all of us. "Right, then," he said briskly. "Thank you all for coming. What can we do to help you with your investigation?"

Tyler opened his mouth to speak, but I spoke up first. "We'd like to ask you some questions," I said. Tyler glared at me, but I ignored him. "We'd also like to talk to any staff members who were here on the night of the party."

"I'll get everyone together," Mrs. Gory offered.

Wendy raised her hand. "Can I use your ladies' room, Mrs. Grory? I need to do a lipstick check."

"Gory," Althea corrected her. She and Chen, who were standing next to each other, exchanged a glance that seemed to say, *Couldn't they have prescreened the contestants for signs of intelligence?*

"Your lipstick looks fine, Wendy. We need to focus," Tyler snapped.

"Whatever," Wendy grumbled.

Within a few minutes, Mrs. Gory had rounded up her staff. We all sat down so we could start the interviews.

Hamish sat down in a high-backed leather chair. He pulled a pipe out of his pocket and put it in his mouth without lighting it. Okay, now that's taking the Sherlock Holmes look a little far, I thought, trying to suppress a smile.

"Let's start from the beginning, shall we?" Hamish said, gesturing with his pipe.

The crew circled us with their cameras, lights, and microphones. Ms. Darby stood in a corner, watching intently.

This was the perfect time for me to use George's microcassette recorder, which was tucked inside my jacket pocket. I felt for the On button and pressed it. It was voice-activated, so it would only record when

44

someone was talking. I also had my notebook and pen on hand, so I could write down the really important stuff.

"Mrs. Gory, tell us what happened, in your own words," I said.

Mrs. Gory smoothed her hair and nodded. "Yes, of course. Let's see. The party had just started. I was in the front hallway, greeting guests. I realized that I had forgotten to put on my beautiful Laurier diamond necklace. I absolutely *had* to wear it with my black evening gown! So I went to the library to get it."

"Hmm, most interesting," Hamish murmured. He gestured at Mrs. Gory with his pipe. "You keep your diamond necklace in the library?"

"We have a safe in the library," Mrs. Gory explained.

"What happened next?" Chen prompted her.

"I went to the library—," Mrs. Gory said.

"Alone?" Althea cut in.

"Alone. I entered the combination and opened the safe. I keep my necklace in a special silver box inside the safe. I opened the box, and the necklace was there. But just then, I heard a scream." Mrs. Gory looked upset.

"Oh, my! How scary!" Mary Lee exclaimed.

Mrs. Gory pointed to the right, toward the back of the house. "The scream had come from the direction of the kitchen. So I closed the silver box and ran to the kitchen. It turned out that one of our maids, Josette, had seen a mouse."

Josette scrunched up her face. "It was very embarrassing," she said in a French-accented voice. "The little rodents, I am very afraid of them."

"I saw the mouse also," Odile, another maid, volunteered. "I thought it was kind of . . . *mignon* . . . cute."

Josette gasped. "Odile, it was not cute!"

The two of them began arguing in French. Mrs. Gory said something to them, also in French, which made them promptly shut up.

Mrs. Gory turned her attention back to the rest of us. "After I made sure everything was okay, I went back to the library," she continued. "I realized then that I had forgotten to lock the safe. I opened the silver box. It was empty! My necklace was gone!"

"How many minutes passed between the time you left the library and the time you got back? Approximately?" I asked her.

"No more than five minutes, I would think. I didn't check the clock, though," Mrs. Gory replied.

Tyler raised his pen in the air. "You said you were in the front hallway greeting guests when you excused yourself to go to the library, Mrs. Gory. How many guests had arrived at this point, and who were they?"

Mrs. Gory looked thoughtful. "Let's see, there were about a dozen people. The party had barely started, and most guests like to arrive to a party fashionably late, you know? There was my good friend Florence Pomeroy." She paused to spell the name. "There was Thierry Devereaux, who was for once in his life *not* with one of his many, many girlfriends. That man! He must spend all of his so-called fortune buying them fur coats and jewelry and an assortment of other—"

"Darling!" Sir Adrian hissed at her.

Mrs. Gory blushed. "Yes, right. I'm sorry, darling. Where was I? Marguerite Mercier was one of the early guests too. A bit of a busybody, if you ask me, but one must invite her to one's parties because she's rather a VIP in town. There was also Sebastien Laroche, Adrian's best friend." She spelled the names of Marguerite Mercier, Sebastien Laroche, and also Thierry Devereaux.

"Sebastien and I work together at the British Embassy," Sir Adrian explained.

"Who were the other guests?" I asked.

"I can put a list together for you," Mrs. Gory offered.

"Mrs. Gory, did any of these dozen guests know you were going to the library to get your necklace?" Wendy piped up.

Mrs. Gory considered this. "Hmm. I was talking to

47

Florence in the front hall when I realized that I had forgotten my necklace. I told her just that, then excused myself and went to the library. I didn't tell anyone else."

Chen leaned forward in his chair. "Mrs. Gory, between the time you excused yourself to go to the library and later, when you came back to the library and found your necklace gone, did you see anyone in the hallway, near the library, or in the library?"

Althea grinned at Chen. "Good question, Li."

Chen grinned back at her. "Thanks, Eisner."

"I don't believe so," Mrs. Gory replied.

"Who knew that you owned this necklace, Mrs. Gory?" Wendy asked her.

Mrs. Gory shrugged. "Oh, well, everyone, I'm sure. I'd worn my beautiful Laurier necklace on several occasions before, at other parties. There was a fabulous picture of me wearing it at the Cormiers' ball in *La Belle Femme* magazine last month, wasn't there, darling?"

Sir Adrian looked startled, as though he hadn't been paying attention to his wife. "Hmm. What, darling?"

"Who knew about this safe?" I asked the couple. "And was anything else taken from it?"

"I don't think anyone knew about the safe besides Adrian and me—and of course our staff. And no, nothing else was taken from it," Mrs. Gory replied.

"The necklace was the only thing in there," Sir Adrian added.

"Where were you during this time, Sir Adrian?" I asked him.

"I was in the living room talking to Sebastien—Mr. Laroche," Sir Adrian replied.

I nodded, considering this. Then I turned to the staff. "Did any of the rest of you see anything odd? Anything at all?"

"No, mademoiselle," Adele, Gabrielle, and Brigitte said in unison. The other two maids, Odile and Josette, shook their heads.

"I did not see anything, no," the cook, Raoul, added in a gruff voice. "I was in the cellar getting vegetables."

I was about to ask another question when I was distracted by Ms. Darby whispering to Elizabeth. The two women were close enough to me that I could hear everything.

"Elizabeth, can you please stop hovering and do something useful, like getting me a glass of water?" Ms. Darby was saying to her assistant producer. "And this time, make sure the ice is crushed. Not cubed. I don't know why you can't get these very important details right."

"Yes, Ms. Darby," Elizabeth said, her cheeks red.

"And please call the spa to confirm my massage

appointment for this evening," Ms. Darby went on.

"Yes, Ms. Darby."

The room had fallen silent. Everyone was listening to the two of them now.

Ms. Darby smiled innocently at all of us. "Please don't mind us. Just talking business."

NANCY'S NOTES, MONDAY

Sequence of events:

* Mrs. Gory was in front hallway talking to friend Florence Pomeroy.

* About a dozen guests had arrived at this point. Included: Florence Pomeroy, Thierry Devereaux, Marguerite Mercier, and Sebastien Laroche (Sir Gory's best bud/work together at Embassy).

* Mrs. G realized she forgot necklace. Excused herself. Went to library safe.

* Opened library safe. Opened silver box; necklace inside. Heard scream direction of kitchen. Left box in safe; left safe unlocked.

* Went to kitchen. Maid Josette saw mouse; maid Odile confirms.

* Mrs. G back to library approx. 5 minutes later. Box still there. Necklace gone.

* Sir Gory talking to Sebastien Laroche in living room during this time.

★ ★ ★

After the interviews were over, the other contestants and I moved over to the library to check out the scene of the crime, followed by Sir Adrian, Mrs. Gory, Dee Darby, Elizabeth, and the crew. I clicked off the tape recorder. The library was more understated than the rest of the townhouse. It was dark brown and woody, with built-in shelves lined with what appeared to be thousands of leather-bound and hardcover books. The books were in alphabetical order, by title, which seemed weird; someone in the Gory house must really be into *order*. Over the mantle was a large portrait of Sir Adrian, posing with a calico cat on his lap. It was the cat I had seen in the living room.

"Where is the safe?" I asked Sir Adrian.

He indicated a painting of a horse next to a large mahogany desk. "Behind here," he said. He removed the painting from the wall, revealing a gunmetal-gray safe door.

He entered the combination, and the door swung open. Tyler stepped forward and was about to reach inside the safe when something occurred to me.

"Wait! Stop!" I cried out.

Tyler turned around and frowned impatiently at me. "What's the problem, Nancy? We don't have all day."

51

"We should dust the inside of the safe for finger-prints," I suggested.

Tyler considered this. "Okay. Not a bad idea."

"Yeah, awesome," Fish agreed.

"But we don't have a fingerprinting kit," Althea pointed out.

I turned to the maid Josette, who was hovering in the doorway. "Could you get me some white talcum powder? Also a makeup brush, some Scotch tape, a flashlight, and a piece of construction paper? The paper should be a dark color, like black or brown—something like that."

Josette curtsied. "*Oui,* mademoiselle." She added, "*Tout de suite,*" which meant, "Right away."

"A makeup brush? Talcum powder?" Mary Lee said, puzzled.

"You're on the wrong reality TV show, Nancy," Wendy joked. "You must think you're on that make-over show, *Ugly Ducklings.*"

"This brings to my mind one of my favorite Sherlock Holmes stories, 'The Adventure of the Priory School,'" Hamish said, gesturing with his unlit pipe. "Except, that case involved cow prints, not fingerprints."

I frowned at Hamish, confused. I wasn't sure what fingerprints had to do with cow prints. I was begin-ning to suspect that Hamish liked talking about

Sherlock Holmes stories even if they were totally un-related to the matter at hand.

"Hey, what's this?" Althea said suddenly.

I glanced in her direction. She was sitting in a brown leather chair near the mantel. I saw her reach down and pick something off the floor. It was small, slender, and shiny.

"Looks like a letter opener," Hamish observed.

Sir Adrian strode over and took it from Althea. "Thank you, that's mine. I must have misplaced it."

Something occurred to me. "Are you sure you misplaced it, Sir Adrian? Maybe our thief used it for some reason. It could be a clue."

"No, no, I'm sure it was me," Sir Adrian replied. "I was sitting in this very chair the other day, opening my mail. I believe I put it down on the floor to answer the telephone."

A few minutes later, Josette appeared with the items I had asked her for, including a piece of black construction paper. I took them and thanked her, then proceeded to the safe.

"What exactly are you doing with all that . . . stuff?" Tyler asked me skeptically.

I didn't answer him. I clicked on the flashlight and swept it in slow arcs around the inside of the safe. There was only one thing inside the safe: a small silver box.

"You said your diamond necklace was inside this silver box, right?" I asked Mrs. Gory.

"Yes," Mrs. Gory replied.

"When you heard the scream, you closed the box but not the safe door before you ran to the kitchen," I confirmed.

"Yes," Mrs. Gory replied again.

I turned back to the safe. Good. This meant that the thief had to open the box in order to retrieve the necklace. Which meant that he—or she—might have left fingerprints somewhere on the box.

I leaned forward as far as I could and scanned the top of the box with the flashlight. Silver was a good surface for capturing fingerprints.

After a moment, I noticed some faint ridges near the clasp. I tried to hide my excitement. That could be them!

I dipped the makeup brush in the talcum powder and dusted the ridges very lightly. I made sure to stroke in the direction of the ridges, which was the right way to lift prints. Gradually, an impression emerged in the field of white powder. Yes!

Then I noticed something else on the box. There were some more faint ridges a few inches over. I dusted them with talcum powder too. It was a second fingerprint!

I felt—or rather, heard—someone breathing nearby.

I turned my head and saw Mary Lee standing really, really close to me. She was writing like mad in her pink notebook and glancing up occasionally to see what I was doing.

"Mary Lee? Could you give me a little room?" I asked her gently.

Mary Lee blushed. "Oh, I am so sorry," she apologized, taking a few steps back. "I was, um, just watching you work. It's so interesting!"

I gave her a quick smile and returned to my task. I tore a generous piece of Scotch tape and pressed it down on the first fingerprint. Then I scraped my thumbnail across the tape. I repeated the procedure with the second fingerprint.

"Wow, Nancy. What are you doing, exactly?" Mary Lee asked, sounding awestruck.

"Yeah, Nancy. We need to move on here," Tyler said impatiently.

I peeled off the tape pieces slowly and stuck them to the black construction paper. I held up the paper.

"We have a clue," I announced. "Two fingerprints. And from what I can tell, they're from two different people."

5

The Enigma

Let's see," **Tyler** said, grabbing the piece of black construction paper from me.

"I want to see too," Wendy said, trying to grab it from Tyler.

A feeding frenzy was erupting over the fingerprint clue. If this kept up, someone was going to end up ripping the evidence in half. "Please be careful with that," I warned. "It's really delicate."

"Yeah, okay, fine," Tyler conceded. He set the construction paper down on the desk, and everyone immediately swarmed around it.

"Wow, is that cool or what," Fish said admiringly. "If you stare at it with your eyes half closed, it kind of looks like two jellyfish swimming in a seaweed forest."

"How can you tell that the fingerprints are from two different people?" Mary Lee asked me.

I pointed to the two white impressions. "See the one on the left? It has an arch pattern. The one on the right has a whorl pattern. You can tell because it has a full circle in the middle. A person can have one pattern or the other, but not both." I added, "There's a third kind of pattern, called a loop pattern, which we're not seeing here. That's actually the most common type."

Chen found a magnifying glass on one of the bookshelves and brought it over. He leaned over the fingerprints and studied them carefully through the glass. "You're right, Nancy. Definitely a loop pattern on the left and a whorl pattern on the right. Two different individuals."

I glanced up at Sir Adrian. "Who has the combination to this safe?" I asked him.

"My wife and myself of course," Sir Adrian replied. "No one else." He added, "Otherwise, you might as well advertise the combination on the front page of the *International Post*. You can't trust people to keep secrets." He made a face.

"We need to make sure these fingerprints aren't yours," I told the couple. "Josette, could you please find us an ink pad and a white piece of paper?"

"*Oui,* mademoiselle," Josette said readily.

When Josette had gotten the supplies, I asked Sir Adrian and his wife to dip their index fingers in the ink.

Mrs. Gory crinkled her nose in distaste. "That sounds so messy."

"Is it really necessary?" Sir Adrian said irritably.

I nodded. "I'm afraid so."

After complaining some more, they finally relented. I took their prints and labeled them: AG INDEX FINGER and GG INDEX FINGER, with the date and time. Using the magnifying glass, I compared them to the fingerprints I'd taken from inside the safe.

"Take a look," I said to Hamish, who was standing next to me.

Hamish peered through the magnifying glass. "Elementary, my dear Watson—I mean, Nancy," he said jovially. "The fingerprints in the safe match Sir Adrian's and Mrs. Gory's fingerprints exactly."

I nodded. "That's right. Which means that our thief was careful not to leave fingerprints—none that I could see, anyway. He or she may have worn gloves."

"So these clues are useless," Wendy grumbled, waving her perfectly manicured nails at the fingerprints on the black construction paper. "We just wasted half an hour."

I glanced at the construction paper—and did a double take. "Or maybe not," I said slowly.

Mary Lee's eyes widened. "What do you mean, Nancy? Did you just solve the mystery, or what?" she said excitedly.

I bent down over the construction paper and studied the piece of Scotch tape with fingerprint number one under it.

There was something there besides the print.

It was a fine red hair.

"No, I didn't solve the mystery," I replied after a moment. "But I did find another clue. Our thief may have been a redhead."

The eight of us—Hamish, Wendy, Chen, Althea, Tyler, Mary Lee, Fish, and I—convened around the Gorys' dining-room table to go over the case so far. Dee Darby stood in the corner, wearing a headset and whispering directions to the crew. Elizabeth stood beside her, scribbling down notes. Jean Alain and two other cameramen circled the table, taping our discussion.

"We need to interview the party guests who were here at the time," Tyler said. "What were their names?"

"Florence Pomeroy, Thierry Devereaux, Marguerite Mercier, and Sebastien Laroche," Althea said, referring to her notebook. "Mrs. Gory is getting us the other eight names, plus addresses for everyone. I also think we should try to—"

"Shouldn't we talk to the police and see if any of them have criminal records?" Wendy spoke up. "That's what they always do on that TV show *Crime Hunters*."

"That is the lamest show, ever," Chen remarked.

"Whatever," Wendy shot back.

"What about the red hair?" I spoke up. "We need to find its owner. Probably the strategy would be for us to—"

Tyler cut me off. "The red hair could be a red herring. Who knows how it got in that safe, or when?"

"Tyler, you shouldn't interrupt Nancy, she's a *real* detective," Mary Lee said, shooting Tyler a look.

"Well, that's not entirely true," I corrected her. "I'm actually more of an amateur detect—"

"I agree with whatever Mary Lee says," Fish said, putting his arm around the back of her chair. Mary Lee blushed.

"Well, the red hair doesn't belong to Sir Adrian or Mrs. Gory or any of their staff, anyway," Althea pointed out.

"Speaking of redheads, there is a fascinating Sherlock Holmes story called 'The Red-Headed League,'" Hamish said. "It has to do with the mysterious activities of a pawnbroker who is paid to go to a certain office every day, to copy the *Encyclopedia Britannica*."

"Okay, Webster? Watson? Whatever your name is?

Could we take a break from the Sherlock Holmes fanfest?" Tyler snapped.

Hamish flushed. "You don't need to be rude."

"If I could get back to the—," I began.

"What if the thief wasn't one of the party guests or on the staff?" Chen interrupted. "What if it was an intruder who slipped inside the house? Or broke in? Is there a security system in this place?"

"Good insight, Li," Althea said, raising her hand and slapping him a high five.

"I think we should think about—," I tried again.

"Like people who have a gazillion-dollar house *aren't* going to have a security system," Wendy said dryly.

Three other people spoke up at once. I sighed. This discussion was going nowhere. With so many strong egos in the room, it was impossible to get a word in edgewise.

"I'm getting a drink of water," I said to no one in particular, then got up and headed for the kitchen. Jean Alain started to follow me with his camera, but I held up my hand. "Honest. I'm just getting a drink of water," I said in a low voice. "If I decide to make a run for it, I'll let you know so you can get it on camera."

Jean Alain grinned and gave me a wink. Then he slipped around a corner and slid his camera off his shoulder. "Guess I'll take five in that case," he whispered. "Just don't tell Darby!"

"Your secret's safe with me," I said.

I went down the hall to the kitchen. The room was empty. It was nice to be alone after all the arguing between the team members and being trailed everywhere by the crew and Dee Darby. I had never solved a mystery under these conditions before. I was going to have to figure out how to be a "team player" with a team full of really aggressive, really opinionated people. I had never solved a *fake* mystery before, either. I got the feeling that the clues would be different than the kind I was used to.

In the kitchen there was a folding table set up with snacks for the team members and the crew. I grabbed a bottle of water off the table and then I slipped my hand into my pocket to check my PDA, in case George had e-mailed me.

The mailbox icon was flashing—along with the number two. The volume was down, so I hadn't realized that two messages had come in.

The first e-mail was from George. STILL WORKING ON IT, it said. HANG IN THERE! I smiled wistfully, missing my friends more than ever. The three of us worked so well as a team. If only the cast of the show could become the same well-oiled machine.

I turned my attention to the second e-mail. The

hairs on the back of my neck stood up when I saw the sender: DOOMSDAY246.

I opened the e-mail quickly. It said:

Trust no one, Nancy Drew.

I stared at the mysterious message. DOOMSDAY246, who could that be? Another contestant?

I reread the message. *Trust no one, Nancy Drew.* It was spooky that they, whoever *they* were, knew my name. It ruled out random spam mail.

"What do they want with me?" I said out loud, to myself.

"Excuse me, Nancy? Am I interrupting you? Oh, I am, aren't I?"

Startled, I turned around and saw Mary Lee standing behind me, plucking nervously at her white skirt. How had she snuck up on me? I hadn't heard a thing. I also noticed that one of the cameramen—not Jean Alain—was hovering in the doorway, taping.

"Oh, hey, Mary Lee. I'm just getting a drink," I replied. I slipped George's PDA into my pocket and glanced self-consciously at the camera. I still wasn't used to having everything I said and did—well, *almost* everything I said and did—captured on tape.

"I wanted to ask you a question," Mary Lee said. She rifled through her pockets and retrieved a folded-up item, which she smoothed out for me to see.

I peered at it. It was the *International Post* article about the theft of the diamond necklace.

"Something's been bugging me," Mary Lee began, jabbing her finger at the article. "Why did Mrs. Gory throw a huge party for Mr. Gory's sixty-first birthday? Aren't huge parties usually for, you know, like, your fiftieth or sixtieth or seventieth birthday? My relatives back in Redsprings like to throw birthday parties for each other. But they only throw huge parties for the important birthdays, like the fiftieth and sixtieth and so forth."

I mulled this over. "You have a point," I said after a moment.

Mary Lee beamed. "I do? Really?"

"Really. Here, let me see that article again."

I scanned the *International Post* story, focusing on the detail about Sir Adrian's birthday:

> "Anyone who can solve this mystery will be generously rewarded," said Sir Adrian, whose 61st birthday was the occasion for the celebration. "You could say that this theft is truly an Enigma."

It *was* kind of weird that Mrs. Gory had thrown a party with over a hundred guests for a sixty-first birthday. It might be nothing, maybe the Gorys had a huge party every year, but it was certainly worth bringing up with the rest of the team. And then something else leaped out at me—something I hadn't noticed before.

Enigma. Why was the word "Enigma" capitalized?

I pointed this out to Mary Lee, who scrunched up her face. "That's real strange," she agreed. "The word 'enigma' means 'puzzle' or 'mystery,' right? It's not a proper noun, so it shouldn't be capitalized."

"No, it shouldn't," I said thoughtfully. "Come on, let's share this stuff with the others."

We returned to the dining room, followed by the cameraman. Tyler, Wendy, Fish, Chen, Althea, and Hamish were talking animatedly about a famous diamond necklace that was stolen in New York City last year.

"Hey, y'all. Nancy and I may have two new clues!" Mary Lee announced, practically jumping up and down.

Tyler looked up. "Yes? What?"

Mary Lee told the group about the items from the *International Post* article. Before she had a chance to finish, however, Wendy held up her hand.

"The sixty-first birthday business is no big deal," Wendy said dismissively. "Mrs. Gory probably just wanted an excuse to throw a big party. She's like my friend Tamara. Tamara is such a party fiend, she'll invite a hundred people over to her house for, you know, like, Arbor Day."

"As for the capital *E* in 'Enigma,' it's clearly just a typo," Tyler said, shuffling through some papers. "Okay, gang, we need to refocus and get back to our discussion about—"

"Wait a second," Chen said. He pulled his copy of the *International Post* article out of his dossier. "I think these girls are on to something."

"What do you mean, Li?" Althea asked him.

Chen pointed to the article. "Enigma with a capital *E*. Among other things, that happens to be the name of a famous cryptographic machine from the early twentieth century."

My heart skipped a beat. "Cryptographic, as in code," I said excitedly. "Maybe that's a message to us. Maybe it's telling us that this article contains a code!"

"And maybe the number sixty-one is part of the code," Chen added.

6

The Graveyard Shift

The eight of us sat at the Gorys' dining-room table, poring over our copies of the *International Post* article and scribbling notes. The Gorys' "maids" had brought us tea, coffee, hot chocolate, and a platter of French pastries. The pastries were not like anything I had ever eaten back home. There were *pains au chocolat*, which were flaky crescent-shaped rolls filled with dark, melted chocolate. There were *choux chantilly*, which were golden puffs filled with custard cream. There were *petits fours,* which were different kinds of delicious, bite-size cakes.

But I didn't really have time to pig out. I was too excited about trying to crack the code. I scanned the *International Post* article for the sixth time and took some notes. Out of the corner of my eye, I saw Dee

Darby saying something to one of the cameramen.

"It's probably not a Caesar cipher, which involves each letter of the code corresponding to a letter further down the alphabet," Chen mused. "It's probably not a Viginere cipher or a Beaufort cipher, either. Of course, the code may not be contained in the words themselves but somewhere else. We should do a check for invisible ink, microdots, and digital watermarks."

"You seem to know a lot about cryptography," I remarked.

Chen shrugged. "One of my hobbies."

I turned my attention back to the article. Chen was right; it probably wasn't the sort of code where each letter represents another letter, since the article made sense as it was. Those kinds of codes usually read like a string of nonsense words: "RBSJT, GS-BODE," instead of "Paris, France," for example.

I tried another approach. Maybe we were supposed to take the first or last letters of each word and string them together. I scanned the first paragraph:

During a lavish birthday party thrown by Gillian Gory for her husband, British diplomat Sir Adrian Gory, a thief or thieves made off with Mrs. Gory's prized diamond necklace.

I picked up a pen and started writing in my note-book: *D, A, L, B, P, T.* I stopped. That was definitely not it. I then tried the last letter of each word: *G, A, H, Y, Y, N.* I stopped again. That wasn't it either.

Okay, so I would cast a wider net. How about the first or last letters of each sentence instead? I started with the letter *D.* Then I read over the rest of the article.

Odile Olivier, one of the Gorys' maids, told the police that the necklace is from Laurier Jewelers, the internationally renowned jewelry store. Reputed to be worth over $1 million U.S., the necklace was taken from the Gorys' safe at their townhouse on Rue de Grenelle just as the party was getting started.

"It all happened so quickly," Olivier said. "All of us were terribly upset. No one more so than Sir Adrian and Madame Gillian of course."

Guests included over a hundred friends, family members, and prominent local citizens, according to a guest list provided by one of the Gorys' staff. Right now, the police have no suspects.

"Anyone who can solve this mystery will be generously rewarded," said Sir Adrian, whose

61st birthday was the occasion for the celebration. "You could say that this theft is truly an Enigma."

O, I wrote. Then *R*, *I*, *A*, *N*. Dorian. That sounded like a person's name! I realized that I could be on to something.

I went to the sentence that began "Guests included . . ." That was *G*. Then *R*, *A*, *Y*.

Dorian Gray. Was that the identity of our thief?

"Who's Dorian Gray?" I said out loud, barely able to contain my excitement.

"Nancy, did you break the code?" Chen demanded.

"I think so," I said. "Was there a Dorian Gray on the invitation list for the party?"

"Uh, like, no," Wendy said, rolling her eyes. "I would have remembered a dorky name like that."

"Dorian Gray. I think he's a boarder from Baja," Fish spoke up.

"Dorky name? Boarder from Baja?" Althea snapped. "Guys, Dorian Gray is the main character in one of the best-known novels of the nineteenth century: *The Picture of Dorian Gray,* by Oscar Wilde."

"A novel?" I said, surprised. "So the code leads us to a novel?"

"Nancy, you are so, so smart!" Mary Lee praised me. "How did you break the code?"

I explained that the first letter of each sentence in the article spelled out the words "Dorian Gray." When I finished, Hamish began clapping. "This is an important breakthrough. Well done, Nancy! And you, too, Althea!"

"Yeah, but now what?" Wendy said, studying her nails. "What does a fictional character have to do with a *real* diamond necklace?"

"I noticed that the Gorys' library had quite a few books," Hamish said. "I suggest we all head over to it posthaste and see if they might have a copy of *The Picture of Dorian Gray*."

"Good idea," I agreed.

We all rushed to the library, followed by the cameras and Dee Darby. Even though we were working as a team, there was still a feeling of competition in the air—who could solve the code first, who could get to the library first, and so on. In fact, we were in such a hurry as we swarmed down the hallway that we practically stepped on the poor little calico cat. She hissed at us and scrambled up the stairs.

Once in the library, Althea was the first one to locate *The Picture of Dorian Gray*. It was sandwiched in between *Pale Fire* by Vladimir Nabokov and *The Portrait of a Lady* by Henry James. As she pulled it off the shelf, I could smell the faint, musty smell of old leather.

"Page sixty-one," I said suddenly. "Check out page sixty-one."

"Yes!" Mary Lee exclaimed. "As in, Mr. Gory's sixty-first birthday."

"Here, let me see that," Tyler said, trying to grab the book away from Althea.

Althea grabbed it back. "Hey! You need to chill out and take a yoga class or something. Let someone take charge for a change."

Chen stepped forward. "Stop hassling her, man," he told Tyler gruffly.

"I can take care of myself, Li," Althea told Chen. "Thanks, anyway."

"No problem, Eisner," Chen replied.

Althea turned her attention back to the book. I peered over her shoulder as she leafed through the pages. "Page sixty-one, page sixty-one," she murmured. "Here we go. Hey, check this out!"

I leaned forward to get a closer look. Page sixty-one looked like all the rest—except for the last two words. They were gibberish:

QFSF MBDIBJTF

"Cool, it's another code!" Fish exclaimed.

"Oscar Wilde definitely didn't write this," Althea agreed.

"Someone must have mocked up this page and inserted the gibberish words as a clue," I said.

"Now, *this* could be a Caesar cipher," Chen spoke up. He pulled a notebook out of his pocket and began scribbling like mad. "Let's see, if you move all the letters down one place in the alphabet . . . no, that doesn't work."

Althea set the book down on Sir Gory's desk and joined Chen. "How about two letters down, Li?" she suggested.

We all got our notebooks out and started trying to decode the two words. After a few minutes, Hamish raised his hand in the air. "I got it, people! You have to move all the letters *up* one place in the alphabet. The answer is *P-E-R-E- L-A-C-H-A-I-S-E*. Père Lachaise."

Wendy frowned. "That can't be right. I've never read anything with any Père Lachaise."

"It's probably something French," Mary Lee suggested.

"The title of another book?" I spoke up.

"Maybe it's the name of a restaurant," Hamish said.

"I think they're an indie band from Montreal," Fish put in.

We went through a few more rounds of this. At one point during the discussion, I heard the front door open and close. I didn't think anything of it until I happened to look up and glance around the room.

Althea and Chen were gone, along with one of the cameramen.

"I can't believe Althea and Chen abandoned us," Wendy complained. "Who do they think they are, anyway?"

"It's part of the game," Tyler pointed out. "Any of us can jump ship at any time. You all watch *Mystery Solved!* back home, right? It happens like a dozen times on every episode."

Wendy, Tyler, Hamish, Fish, Mary Lee, and I were standing at the front entrance of Père Lachaise, on the Boulevard Ménilmontant. It had taken us nearly an hour to figure out that Père Lachaise was a famous cemetery in the twentieth arrondissement. We finally found a reference to it in a Paris guidebook in the library. We had immediately left the Gorys' house and hailed cabs to get us there.

It was almost five o'clock. The twilight sky was streaked with gold and pink. The cobblestoned street was lined with pretty old brownstones, tiny shops, and cafés. People rushed home along the sidewalks, carrying briefcases, bags of groceries, and fresh baguettes wrapped in white paper. Most of them stared at us as we proceeded into the cemetery. I realized we must be quite a spectacle: the six of us, TV cameras, Dee Darby, and assorted crew members.

On the other side of the large stone gate there was a wide path lined with hundreds of gravestones. Some were small and simple, just slabs of stone. Others were large and ornate, with elaborate fountains or statues in honor of the dead. Many of them were so old and crumbling, you could barely make out the inscriptions.

I had never been to such a huge cemetery before. It was like being in a city of graves.

"Okay, gang, this is a pretty big place," Hamish said, gesturing with his pipe. "The guidebook said it was over a hundred acres, right? So where do we start?"

"There has to be a clue here somewhere," I agreed. "But where?"

"I found a map of the cemetery in the guidebook," Mary Lee said helpfully. "I brought it with me." She pulled the book out of her bag and started flipping through the pages. "Here it is. Wow, there's a whole bunch of famous people buried here."

"Really? Anyone I'd know?" Wendy said dryly.

"'Famous musicians include Rossini, Bizet, and Chopin,'" Mary Lee read out loud. "Hey, my piano teacher makes me play Chopin."

"Can I hear you play the piano sometime, Mary Lee?" Fish asked her. "I could sing along or something. You know, I compose songs in my spare time."

"We need to focus on the mystery, Fish," Mary

Lee told him. She continued reading. "It says there are famous politicians buried here too, and dancers, and writers."

This caught my attention. "Writers? Like who?" I asked her.

Mary Lee turned the page. "Um, here we go. How do you pronounce this: Honoré de Balzac? Colette, no last name. Marcel Proust. Gertrude Stein. Oscar—hey, Oscar Wilde!" she cried out. "Isn't that the guy who wrote the Dorian Gray book?"

"Oscar Wilde is buried here?" Tyler asked her intently.

Mary Lee nodded. "Yup. His grave is in . . . hmm . . . section eighty-nine of the cemetery. Right now, we're in between sections one and two. Wow, we have a *long* way to go, y'all."

"We'd better hurry, then," Tyler said, picking up the pace. "Come on, people! Althea and Chen have an hour's head start!"

We hurried after Tyler, and Ms. Darby, the cameramen, and the crew hurried after us. Eventually, the cemetery curved up a hillside. The graves were organized along dozens of paths with names like Chemin du Dragon, Avenue Transversale, and Chemin des Anglais. Along the way, we passed several small groups of tourists snapping photographs—I overheard snatches of Italian, German, and Japanese. Otherwise, we seemed to have the place to ourselves at this late hour.

"Am I doing okay?" Mary Lee whispered to me as we turned onto Avenue Aguado.

"You're doing *great*," I said encouragingly. "You're a natural detective."

Mary Lee beamed. "Wow, thanks so much, Nancy! That's a huge compliment, coming from you."

We eventually reached Oscar Wilde's grave, which was on Avenue Transversale 3 between Avenue Aguado and Avenue Carette. It was a large stone structure with the shape of a winged creature—maybe something from Greek mythology—carved into it. There were vases of fresh and wilting flowers everywhere. Offerings from fans, I assumed.

I knelt down and studied the base of the head-stone close up. Oscar Wilde's name was engraved along the front.

And then I noticed something else. There were strange marks all over the grave. They looked like . . . lipstick prints? Was that possible?

"Am I imagining things, or do these look like lip-stick prints to you?" I said to the rest of the group.

Mary Lee knelt down beside me, her face bent over the open guidebook. "It says here that Oscar Wilde's fans often kiss his grave when they visit it. The lipstick prints are a tradition." She crinkled her nose. "That's kind of weird, isn't it? Kissing a grave?"

Wendy knelt down between Mary Lee and me. She pointed to a bright purplish red lipstick mark near the right edge of the gravestone. It looked fresh.

"You can tell that Ms. Althea Know-It-All's been here," Wendy said. "I recognize her lipstick color. It's *so* last year."

"That means that Althea and Chen were definitely here before us," Tyler said with a frown. "That's not good."

"Maybe they found the diamond necklace already," Fish spoke up. "I mean, what if the thief buried it here or something?"

I glanced at the ground around the grave. "There's no freshly dug earth here, so that's probably not the case," I said after a moment. "Still, there might have been an important clue. It's possible that Althea and Chen found it before us."

"And now it's gone, and they're gone," Hamish sighed. "This reminds me of another Sherlock Holmes story. . . ."

As Hamish talked, I thought about this latest turn of events. If Althea and Chen did come across a clue, then they were one step ahead of us. So unless the pair was willing to share their intel, the six of us were at a dead end—except for that mysterious red hair.

Now what?

7

A Spy in the Midst

T hat night, **Dee Darby** arranged for Hamish, Wendy, Tyler, Fish, Mary Lee, and I to have dinner at the Café Josephine, which was one of the restaurants in the Hotel Royale. We were the only diners, which gave us privacy to discuss the case. Jean Alain and another cameraman were there, taping our discussion. Ms. Darby herself left after a few minutes, saying she had an errand to run.

I had never eaten at such a fancy restaurant. The walls of the dining room were covered with mirrors, which glowed warmly with the reflection of candle-light. We sat in leather booths around black and silver tables. Waiters hovered discreetly, pouring us drinks and handing us menus that were entirely in French.

"What's . . . *ris de veau*?" Hamish said, squinting at the menu. "I've never heard of that."

"That's a rice dish," Tyler said immediately. "I eat in French restaurants all the time. Business lunches with clients. You could say that I'm kind of an expert when it comes to French cuisine."

"What are you having, Tyler?" Mary Lee asked him.

"I'm having the escargots. That's a special French casserole made with chicken and vegetables," Tyler replied, snapping his menu shut.

"Sounds yummy," Wendy said. "I think I'll have that too."

I noticed that Jean Alain was looking strangely at Tyler. I wondered why. But before I had a chance to ask him, the waiter came by and took all our orders. I finally decided on *moules frites*: mussels with a side of french fries.

"This restaurant reminds me of Suki's Shrimp Shack, back home," Fish said wistfully. "Suki's has the best shrimp and pineapple kebabs in all of Waikiki. And on Friday nights, they have this awesome poetry slam—"

"Let's get back to business, shall we?" Tyler said abruptly. "Who are our suspects so far?"

"No one," Hamish muttered to me.

"I have a theory," Wendy spoke up. She was dressed in a glamorous-looking metallic-blue dress. I was still wearing the same khaki pants and black sweater that I'd been wearing all day. Bess would definitely not approve.

"What's your theory, Wendy?" I asked.

"What if that maid who saw the mouse, Josette, is our thief?" Wendy said slowly. "I mean, one of our thieves? Maybe she was working with a partner. Maybe she screamed at just the right time so Mrs. Gory would leave the library and run to the kitchen. Then her partner snuck into the library and stole the necklace." Wendy sat back in her chair with a smug expression.

"That's actually not a bad theory," Tyler said.

"I agree," I said. Wendy obviously knew about more than clothes and makeup. "The only problem is that Josette really did see a mouse. That other maid, Odile, confirmed it."

"So maybe Josette was carrying a mouse in a tiny little pet carrier and released it at just the right time," Wendy suggested. "Or maybe Odile was involved as well and lied about the mouse."

"*Three* partners in crime," Fish remarked. "Whoa, that's intense."

We continued discussing the case and our strategy for the next day until the food arrived. Tyler frowned at his thick earthenware plate, which had twelve small holes in it. There was something brown and bubbling in the holes. "What . . . is . . . this?" he asked the waiter. "I didn't order this. I ordered escargots."

"These are escargots, monsieur," the waiter said patiently. "Snails in garlic and butter."

"Snails?" Wendy hissed at Tyler. "You ordered us *snails*?"

"Obviously there's been some sort of mistake," Tyler mumbled.

"Here, you can have some of my chicken—there's a lot here," Hamish offered graciously.

Just then, the front door of the restaurant opened with a tinkling of bells. Chen and Althea walked in, followed by Dee Darby, Elizabeth, and one of the cameramen from the show.

It occurred to me right then that Ms. Darby had suggested this restaurant to Chen and Althea, knowing that the rest of us were eating here. Maybe she had been hoping to start some sort of confrontation between the two defectors and the team they'd left behind. More and more, I was beginning to realize that "reality" TV wasn't so real. People like Ms. Darby obviously did a lot of manipulating behind the scenes.

Hamish stood up in his seat. "Chen! Althea! Over here!" he called out in a friendly voice.

Chen and Althea turned. They seemed surprised to see us all here. Chen whispered something in Althea's ear, and they walked over.

"Hey," Chen greeted us. "How's the food here?"

"Fantastic," Hamish said. "Slimy," Wendy said at the same time.

"Do you want to join us?" Hamish offered. "We could get two more chairs over here. Excuse me, waiter!"

"You don't need to bother," Althea said. "We're not staying."

"Oh, please do!" Mary Lee pleaded. "We would love to hear about your trip to the cemetery today. Did y'all find any clues?" she added with a wink.

Chen smiled slyly. "Nice try. I'm afraid we can't answer that."

Tyler reached into his pocket and pulled out a gold money clip stuffed with folded-up bills. "I'll give you five hundred dollars for whatever clue you found at Oscar Wilde's grave," he offered. "If the clue pans out, I'll give you another five hundred dollars. That's one thousand dollars, total. You can't say no to that."

I noticed Dee Darby in the background, gesturing to Jean Alain and the other cameramen to move in closer to our table. Elizabeth was frantically writing notes onto a clipboard.

"Thanks for the, um, generous offer, but we have to turn it down," Althea told Tyler. "Chen and I've found it more efficient to . . . work alone."

"Yeah," Chen said. "Definitely."

Chen and Althea bid us good-bye, then left the restaurant. The same cameraman who had trailed them in followed them out.

"Well, that wasn't very friendly of them," Mary Lee complained.

"Nancy! Nancy Drew!"

I glanced up. Ms. Darby was waving at me to come over. I dabbed at my lips with a napkin and stood up. "I'll be right back," I said to the others.

I walked over to Ms. Darby. I wondered what she wanted.

"Follow me," she instructed.

She led me out of the main dining room, into what appeared to be a small, private dining room next door. There was a cameraman and a couple of other crew members there, fussing over equipment. The doors closed behind us.

Ms. Darby gestured to one of the crew members, who clipped a tiny microphone to my sweater.

"Wait a second," I began. "What's going—"

"Time for a 'Candid Confessions' segment," Ms. Darby cut in. The cameraman turned his video camera on and pointed it at me.

"Nancy Drew! Any comments on your conversation with Althea and Chen just now?" Ms. Darby asked me in her interviewer voice. "How do you feel now that you, Hamish, Wendy, Mary Lee, Fish, and

Tyler have apparently fallen into second place behind the two of them?"

I stared at Ms. Darby, speechless. I hadn't expected to be yanked away from dinner for this. I felt as though I had been ambushed. But I knew I didn't have a choice; I had to participate. Ms. Darby had made that clear this morning. I took a deep breath and tried to think of how to reply.

"Um, well, I'm not sure we've fallen into second place," I said slowly. "Uh, we're pretty sure that Althea and Chen reached Oscar Wilde's grave before we did. But we don't know for certain that they found anything there."

"What do you think of Tyler? Is he too bossy?" Ms. Darby said, abruptly changing the subject.

"Tyler?" I hesitated, trying to think of a polite response. I wasn't going to let Ms. Darby bait me into saying anything catty or mean. "Tyler's very sure of himself," I said after a minute.

"What about Mary Lee? She seems kind of inexperienced in the mystery-solving department, doesn't she? Some people might even say *clueless*." Ms. Darby grinned at her own joke.

"Mary Lee seems really motivated," I said.

"And what about Fish? Is he out to lunch, or what?"

"Fish seems really sweet."

"What's up with Hamish's Sherlock Holmes act,

anyway? Do you think he takes himself a little *too* seriously?"

"Hamish is a big mystery fan."

"And how about that Wendy? Some people might say that she just wants to be on TV. What do you think, Nancy?"

"I don't know what her motives are. But she seems pretty smart."

Ms. Darby fired a few more questions at me. It was clear that she was trying to get me to say something—*anything*—nasty about my fellow contestants.

I didn't give in, but as she wrapped up the interview, I realized that she was going to do the exact same thing to Hamish, Mary Lee, and the others.

Would one of *them* say nasty things about *me*?

When I returned to the main dining room, the other contestants were gone. Hamish had left me a note scribbled on a napkin: *We're all going to bed. See you tomorrow 8 a.m.* Jean Alain was packing up his camera. Elizabeth was sitting at a corner table, scribbling into a notebook. She glanced up when she saw me and waved wearily. I waved back.

Ms. Darby breezed past me. She was talking on her cell phone in rapid-fire French. "Good work today," she called out to me, then breezed out of the restaurant.

The waiters were clearing away the dishes. I

picked up my purse and started to head for the door when I felt a hand on my arm.

I turned around. It was Jean Alain.

"Listen, are you doing anything now?" he asked me with a friendly smile. "I'm officially off duty. I thought it might be fun for us to go for a walk. I can show you the real Paris," he added.

I stared at him in surprise. Jean Alain had barely said a dozen words to me since I had arrived at the hotel yesterday. Was he asking me out on a date?

Of course I had to say no. I was exhausted from the day, and I was still recovering from jet lag. I wanted to go up to my hotel room and mull over the case, alone. And most important, I wasn't in the market for dating anyone, even if Jean Alain *was* a cute French guy. After all, I had the world's greatest boyfriend back home, Ned Nickerson.

"Listen, Jean Alain—," I began.

Jean Alain leaned closer to me and lowered his voice. "There's something you should know about one of the other contestants," he whispered.

I started. He had my attention. One of the other contestants! Could this have something to do with the strange e-mails?

"Well, maybe a short walk," I agreed.

Jean Alain's smile grew wider. "*Très bien,*" he said, touching my elbow. "Come on, let's get out of here."

As we walked out the door together, I couldn't help notice that someone was watching us.

It was Elizabeth. She was staring intently at Jean Alain.

What's that about? I wondered.

Jean Alain and I walked west along the Seine River. The dark water shimmered with the lights of the city and rippled with the reflections of the old bridges that connected the Left Bank and the Right Bank. We passed cafés and restaurants that were bustling with people even at this late hour; tiny outside tables were filled with customers. There were many couples strolling on the sidewalk, arm in arm, laughing. Cars bumped along the cobblestoned street. Lively jazz music poured out of an open apartment window. I finally felt like I was really and truly in Paris.

If only Ned were here, I thought, missing him. We would have such a blast together in this beautiful, romantic city.

"—and so my parents and my brothers and I moved here from Algeria when I was six," Jean Alain was saying. "I really love it here. My apartment is about the size of a shoe box, and my car is older than my grandmother. But otherwise, no complaints. Paris is a wonderful city to live in, especially for people like me who want to go into filmmaking someday."

"How do you like working in television?" I asked him.

Jean Alain shrugged. "It's fine. I freelance, so I pick up jobs here and there. I do a lot of work for *Mystery Solved!* Whenever Darby shoots an episode in Europe, she uses me as a cameraman. I've also done golf tournaments and toothpaste commercials. Not the most fascinating jobs, but, *c'est la vie*," he added with a chuckle. "That's life." He paused and touched my elbow. "Here, let's cross the street."

We made our way across, and Jean Alain led us down a narrow side street lined with tiny shops that were closed for the night. After a few blocks, we turned a corner. Suddenly we found ourselves before an expanse of open park, with trees and grass and flowers and benches.

I gasped, delighted. In the middle of the park was the Eiffel Tower. It was lit up with a thousand twinkling lights and looked totally magical.

"Welcome to Paris," Jean Alain said, grinning. "This is beautiful, no?"

"It's *amazing*," I agreed. "I wish my friends Bess and George were here to see this."

"This park is called the Champs du Mars," Jean Alain explained. "It was built in the eighteenth century. It's one of the most popular spots in Paris, for obvious reasons." He nodded at the Eiffel Tower.

"It's amazing," I repeated, meaning it. It was a breathtaking sight.

I realized suddenly that Jean Alain was standing really, really close to me. He touched my face and leaned in with closed eyes and puckered lips.

I stepped back and smiled apologetically. "I'm flattered. Really. But I have a boyfriend back home," I explained.

Jean Alain's eyes shot open, but he smiled back and pulled away. "No problem," he said cheerfully. "I understand. Your boyfriend is a lucky guy."

I cleared my throat, wanting to change the subject. "Listen, about the other contestants," I began. "You said you had something to tell me about one of them."

Jean Alain's expression grew serious. "That's right," he said gravely. "But first, you have to promise not to tell anyone else."

"Sure," I said, more curious than ever. "What is it?"

Jean Alain glanced over his shoulder, as if to make sure we weren't being overheard. He lowered his voice. "One of the contestants in the show isn't a real contestant," he said.

I gasped. "What?"

"The person is a mole," Jean Alain announced. "A spy."

8

Restless Sleep

I **stared at Jean** Alain in astonishment. "You're saying that one of the other seven people isn't a real contestant?" I said slowly.

Jean Alain nodded. "*Oui*, I'm afraid so."

This wasn't the news I was expecting. My mind began to race. I had a million questions. "Who is it?" I demanded. "What sort of mole? And why would Dee Darby do this? Is it to throw us off course?"

"I'm afraid I don't know any more than what I just told you," Jean Alain replied. "I happened to overhear that there *was* a mole—that's all. Darby is *très* careful about the show's secrets." He paused. "I shouldn't be having this conversation with you, Nancy. I could get fired. So please, please don't tell anyone I told you—especially Darby. I beg you."

He clasped his hands and looked at me with pleading eyes.

I was silent. I didn't know what to say. Jean Alain's revelation had really taken me by surprise.

I also felt guilty. Jean Alain shouldn't be giving me insider information. It was an unfair advantage. For a second, I considered telling the other contestants, just to level the playing field.

But I didn't want to get Jean Alain fired. And if Jean Alain was right and there really *was* a mole, I didn't want to tip my hand to that person.

I went through the other seven contestants in my mind, one by one. I tried to imagine each of them as a mole, spying on the rest of us. Hamish. Mary Lee. Fish. Wendy. Tyler. Chen. Althea. They all seemed like regular people—just like me. But one of them was pretending. Who could it be?

Jean Alain's voice cut into my thoughts. "I told you this secret because I like you, Nancy, and I want to see you win. But I also wanted to warn you. Now that you know there's a mole, you need to be more careful than ever."

"What do you mean?" I asked him.

"I mean, *you can't trust anyone.*"

My eyes opened wide with surprise. Jean Alain's words were the same as the last mysterious e-mail from DOOMSDAY246. *Trust no one, Nancy Drew.*

"Are you DOOMSDAY246" I asked him suddenly.

"Am I . . . what?" Jean Alain looked totally baffled.

"DOOMSDAY246. Did you send me an e-mail using that name?" I persisted.

Jean Alain chuckled. "E-mail? That's very funny. I am—how do you say it?—behind the times. I don't own a computer, and I have no idea how to use e-mail. I prefer to use the telephone to stay in touch with my friends." He added, "But I'm curious. What did this message from this "doomsday" person say?"

I opened my mouth to speak, then clamped it shut. Jean Alain was right. I couldn't trust anyone—and that included him.

"Never mind," I said. "It's not important."

Jean Alain regarded me. "When I said you can't trust anyone, I meant, anyone else besides me," he said, as if reading my mind. "Me and Elizabeth."

"Elizabeth?" I said, surprised.

"She and I are friends," Jean Alain explained. "We like to look out for each other on the show. And we like to look out for people like you. We get very angry at the way Darby treats her contestants. So unfair! The business with the mole is just another example of what she is capable of." He added, "You do not know this, but on the Rome episode of *Mystery Solved!*, Darby slipped false clues to one of the contestants because she didn't like him. He should have won, but he lost."

"You're kidding," I said.

"No, Nancy, I am not kidding. So, like I said: You must be careful. And you must let Elizabeth and me help you if you ever find yourself in trouble. We are on your side."

Back in my hotel room, I put on my favorite pair of pajamas, slipped under the covers, and clicked off the light. It was after midnight. Every cell in my body was beyond exhausted. I couldn't wait to close my eyes and sink into a deep sleep for the next eight hours. . . .

But I couldn't sleep.

I sat up and clicked the light back on. Snippets of the day were flashing through my brain, and I couldn't turn them off. People, conversations, and events were swirling around, competing for my waking attention. I thought about the team's visit to the town house on Rue de Grenelle. I thought about Sir Adrian, Mrs. Gory, Josette, Odile, and the other staff. The two fingerprints. The red hair. The fact that neither Sir Adrian nor Mrs. Gory—nor any of their staff—had red hair. The code in the *International Post* article and the other code in *The Picture of Dorian Gray*. Chen and Althea abruptly leaving the team. Père Lachaise and Oscar Wilde's lipstick-covered grave. The dinner at the fancy restaurant and Chen and Althea walking in. The stroll I took with Jean Alain afterward, and what he told me about the mole—and about Dee Darby.

What was the purpose of the mole? I wondered. Was he or she there to spy, or sabotage, or both? And just who *was* the mole, anyway? I considered my fellow contestants again. Hamish seemed too goofy and earnest to be a spy. On the other hand, his whole Sherlock Holmes obsession could be a cover. Wendy seemed more interested in clothes and makeup than mysteries, but that could be a cover too. In fact, it had occurred to me that she might be a lot smarter than she let on. Mary Lee seemed too sweet and innocent—but again, that could be a cover. Fish's surf-boy persona—ditto. Mr. Alpha Male, Tyler, could certainly be a mole too.

But what about Althea and Chen? They had gone renegade. How could you be a mole without being part of the main team? I supposed anything was possible, though.

I had to consider that any *one* of my seven fellow contestants might be the mole until I had evidence to the contrary. Guilty until proven innocent. Which meant that I couldn't share Jean Alain's news with any of them. I had promised him I wouldn't tell anyone, anyway. If the word spread, he could be fired.

I was no longer sure of the rules of the game. On

the one hand, I didn't feel right accepting insider information from Jean Alain, like about the mole. I shouldn't be letting him or Elizabeth help me, even though they meant well. It seemed like an unfair advantage.

On the other hand, there was nothing in the official *Mystery Solved!* rules that said I *couldn't* talk to anyone working on the show. And if Dee Darby played as dirty as Jean Alain had suggested—feeding false clues to a contestant on the Rome episode— then it seemed as though *anything* was fair.

Besides, Hamish, Mary Lee, and the rest of us were a team. If we *stayed* a team, then anything I knew would help them as well. . . .

I was starting to feel sleepy again. All this thinking was tiring! I reached over and clicked off the light and sank into the big, soft pillows. I yawned . . . and then something started beeping. I bolted up and clicked the light back on. It was George's PDA, which I had left on the dresser.

I got up and hurried across the room. The PDA continued to beep. I picked it up and pressed some buttons. There was an e-mail from George:

```
No luck tracking down the identity of
Doomsday246. He/she didn't leave a
clean, clear electronic trail but
```

```
instead routed the e-mail through
multiple complex networks. Obviously
a computer expert. Sorry. Hope you're
having better luck solving *your*
mystery!
Love, George
```

I sighed, disappointed that George hadn't been able to find anything. There were no new messages from DOOMSDAY246, though; maybe my e-mail stalker had given it a rest. I sent George a quick reply thanking her, then went back to bed. I clicked off the light.

"Sleep, take two," I said out loud, chuckling.

There was a knock on the door.

I clicked the light back on. I glanced at the alarm clock; it was almost 1:00 a.m. Who could be visiting me at this late, late, *late* hour? I wondered.

"Who is it?" I called out.

"Nancy, it's Tyler," came the reply.

What did *he* want? I got up and grabbed a white robe that was hanging on the closet door and slipped it on over my pajamas; it was the complimentary robe, with the words "Hotel Royale" embroidered in delicate gold script across the front. I opened the door.

Tyler was standing in the hallway. He was dressed in

the hotel robe too, over his blue pinstriped pajamas.

"You're wide awake too, huh?" Tyler said. "We detectives never sleep, do we?"

"Well, actually—," I began.

"I'll get right to the point," Tyler interrupted. He slipped his hand into the pocket of his robe and pulled out his gold money clip. "I'll give you five hundred dollars if you leave the group and pair up with me. You and I would definitely win as a duo. What do you say, Nancy? Do we have a deal?"

I stared at him, stunned. "You're offering me money to join up with you?" I said finally.

"Not 'money': five hundred dollars," Tyler corrected me. "You can't say no to that."

"Look, I'm flattered," I said. "But I can't take your money. And I think I'll stick with the rest of the team, for now."

"Okay, you drive a hard bargain. A thousand dollars, and that's my final offer," Tyler persisted.

I shook my head. "No, thanks."

"You're making the biggest mistake of your life," Tyler said, frowning. "Think of how many pairs of fancy French shoes you could buy with a thousand dollars."

"I'm not a huge fan of fancy shoes," I admitted. "But thanks, anyway. Good night."

Tyler left and I closed the door. He was quite a

character, I thought. He was convinced that money could buy him anything . . . unless it was all an act, I reminded myself. Tyler could be the mole, determined to spy on the rest of us, sabotage our efforts, or just spice up the show.

I slipped into bed for the third time that night and drew the warm blankets around me, like a cocoon. I had forgotten to take the robe off, but I didn't care. I was so tired. I clicked the light off . . .

. . . then right back on again when I heard more knocking on the door.

"My answer's still no!" I exclaimed irritably to Tyler.

"Nancy?"

It was a woman's voice. So it wasn't Tyler, after all. Sighing, I got up and padded to the door.

"Who is it?" I called out.

"It's Wendy. Wendy Garcia."

I opened the door. Wendy was standing in the hallway, dressed in red silk pajamas and matching robe. She wasn't wearing makeup, and her face looked like it was covered in shiny goo.

"It's this new cream I bought today," Wendy explained when she saw me staring. "It's made out of honey, avocado oil, green tea, vitamins, wild flowers, and eight different kinds of tropical fruit. It cost a fortune, but it's worth it."

"That's great," I said, wondering why she was

telling me about her new face cream at one in the morning.

Wendy smiled. "Look, I was thinking that we girls have to stick together," she began. "What do you say you and me ditch the rest of this obnoxious so-called team and work together?" She added, "I'd ask Mary Lee, too, but I don't trust her. It's that simple-country-girl act of hers. I'm not buying it. But I have a good feeling about you, Nancy. You're definitely trust-worthy."

"Well, uh, thanks," I said. "I'm really flattered. But I think I want to stay with the team. For now, anyway."

Wendy shrugged. "Okay. It's your choice. If you change your mind, let me know." She stepped closer and squinted at my face. "You know, I think you're starting to get some stress lines. Do you want to bor-row my face cream?"

"No, thanks," I said. I bid her good night and closed the door. I wondered: Could *she* be the mole? She was an actress, after all. She had lots of ex-perience pretending to be something she wasn't. Ms. Darby might have hired her to fill the role.

Yawning, I walked back to the bed, lay down, and clicked off the light—and prayed for some peace and quiet.

9

The Reluctant Redhead

The next morning, there was a note under the door of my room. Actually, "memo" would be more accurate. It was from Tyler, and it had been typed and printed out on the Hotel Royale stationery:

```
TO: Nancy, Mary Lee, Hamish, and Fish
CC: Wendy
FROM: Tyler J. Cox
RE: Today's schedule
    Immediately after the 8 a.m. "Clue
Challenge" segment with Dee Darby, the
four of you are to meet in the hotel
lobby. Your assignment is to visit the
dozen "early-bird" party guests on the
```

list provided by Mrs. Gory and her staff and conduct interviews. These guests were all at the party when the necklace was stolen, so at the moment, they should all be considered possible suspects. They may also provide important information about time line, who was where in the house, etc., leading up to the theft.

Wendy and I will pursue the Oscar Wilde angle; the red hair clue; the clue from yesterday's "Clue Challenge"; and whatever new clue we get at this morning's "Clue Challenge."

Let's all meet back in the hotel lobby at 5 p.m.

The memo was signed with Tylor's big, sweeping initials.

"Ooooo-kay, Mr. Control Freak," I said, chuckling.

I checked the clock. It was seven fifteen. I had already showered and dressed. It was time to head downstairs for my hair and makeup session, and then the second "Clue Challenge."

As I walked to the elevator, I wondered why Tyler had decided to pursue the Oscar Wilde angle. It seemed to be a dead end, since Althea and Chen had gotten to Oscar Wilde's grave before us. If there *had* been a clue there, Althea and Chen had no doubt gotten to it first.

On the other hand, it probably wasn't a bad idea to try again—or maybe try another route. The *International Post* clue had pointed to Oscar Wilde as being a piece of the solution. There might be another way to get more information on Oscar Wilde and ways he might be connected to the missing diamond necklace.

I was glad Tyler had decided to pursue the red hair clue. That was an important one. I couldn't help feeling that the thief was a redhead who had accidentally left his—or her—hair sample at the scene of the crime. It would also be interesting to see if he and Wendy came up with any new ideas about the "ART" clue from yesterday's "Clue Challenge."

When I stepped into the elevator, Fish was there. He was dressed in baggy shorts and a T-shirt with a picture of palm trees on it—not exactly a fall outfit.

"Hey, Nancy Drew," he said cheerfully. "Just the person I wanted to see."

"Really? Why?" I asked him.

For a moment, I thought that he, too, might ask me to leave the team and pair up with him, just as Tyler and Wendy had done last night. I began mentally preparing to give my "I'm flattered, but no thank you" speech yet again.

Fish glanced around, as if to make sure that no one could overhear us—which was kind of silly, since we were alone in an elevator. "I'm glad we're away from the cameras," he said in a low voice. "It's about Mary Lee. I think she's the one, Nancy."

"The . . . one?" I repeated. What was he talking about? Did he know about the mole too? Who could have told him? How did he know that *I* knew? And what made him think Mary Lee was the mole?

"The one," Fish said. He put his hands over his heart. "The woman I've been waiting for all my life."

I stared at him and bit my lip, resisting the impulse to burst out laughing.

"That's . . . great, Fish," I said. "I'm really happy for you."

Fish sighed. "The problem is, she doesn't seem to see it that way. I've asked her out, I've written her love poems. I've even serenaded her outside her hotel room with a song I composed for her, called 'Come Ride with Me on the Surfboard of Love.' But she still won't give me the time of day." He gazed at me hopefully. "She really looks up to you, though. So I thought you might give me some advice on how to win her over."

"I'm not exactly a romance expert," I told him. "Mysteries are more my thing." When I saw Fish's crestfallen expression, I quickly added, "But if I think of anything, I'll let you know. Right away."

Fish smiled. "Thank you! Thank you so much, Nancy! If this all works out I'm going to write a poem in your honor."

"That's cool, Fish. Thanks."

When Fish and I got out of the elevator, we spotted Hamish and Mary Lee in the lobby. Hamish was dressed in his usual Sherlock Holmes garb. Mary Lee was dressed in a purple coat and matching hat. They were walking toward the Savoie Room.

Fish and I sped up to catch them. Out of the corner of my eye, I saw a cameraman hoist his video camera onto his shoulder and race to intercept us. I realized that he was going to tape our conversation. Watch what you say, Drew, I told myself.

"The only real woman in Sherlock Holmes's life was Irene Adler, who appears quite notably in a story called 'A Scandal in Bohemia,'" Hamish was saying to Mary Lee. "Sherlock Holmes was careful to avoid romantic entanglements. He felt that they clouded objectivity."

"Hey, Mary Lee," Fish said, rushing to her side. "You look beautiful today."

"Good morning," Hamish greeted us.

"Oh, hey—you, too, Hamish," Fish said, still staring at Mary Lee.

"Why, thank you. I don't think anyone's ever called me beautiful before," Hamish joked.

Mary Lee turned to me, shaking her head and looking exasperated. She pulled a piece of paper out of her purse. I recognized Tyler's memo. "Hey, Nancy. Did you get one of these too?" she asked.

I nodded. "Yup. I guess we all did."

"So are we taking orders from Mr. I'm-in-Charge?" Mary Lee asked. "Speaking for myself, I'm getting a little tired of his bossy ways."

I shot Mary Lee a warning glance and pointed discreetly to the cameraman behind us. I wanted to let her know that we weren't alone. "I think Tyler means well," I said in a loud voice. "Besides, it *is* a good idea to interview the party guests. We should do it."

Hamish tipped his Sherlock Holmes cap. "I agree with Nancy," he said.

"But Tyler can't treat us like this!" Mary Lee persisted. "I don't know if I want to be on his team anymore."

"If you leave this team, I'm leaving with you," Fish said quickly.

I sighed. This was only day two, and already things were *not* going well—at least in the team spirit department.

It was almost eight o'clock when Anaïs was done with my hair and makeup. As I headed into the Savoie

Room, I touched my face gingerly and winced at the gooey foundation and cream.

The other contestants were already in the room, standing around and talking. Dee Darby, Elizabeth, Jean Alain, two other cameramen, and half a dozen assorted crew members were there as well, setting up.

Jean Alain spotted me walking in. He winked at me and gave me a thumbs-up sign. Then he leaned over to Elizabeth and whispered something.

"Elizabeth!" Ms. Darby burst out. "Please stop your mindless gossiping and pay attention. I've told you this a thousand times. I need the hotel kitchen to make my café au lait with *soy* milk, not *skim* milk. Got it?" She thrust a tall white mug at Elizabeth, spilling coffee onto Elizabeth's shoes.

"Got it, Ms. Darby," Elizabeth said, blushing. She took the mug and rushed off.

"The things I have to endure," Ms. Darby muttered, loudly enough for everyone to hear. "Okay. Places, people! We're going to start taping in sixty seconds."

We all hurried to sit down. I pulled a notebook and pen out of my pocket, just in case. I wondered if today's challenge, like yesterday's, would involve a word puzzle.

The cameramen took their places. Lights clicked on. Elizabeth was not back yet, so Ms. Darby had a young woman named Deirdre pass out folded-up sheets of paper to the other contestants and me.

"This is your 'Clue Challenge' puzzle for the day," Ms. Darby announced. "Whoever solves it first will get this clue to the mystery." She held up a blue envelope.

I unfolded the sheet of paper, my fingers flying. On it were written three words:

HER RED RING

I frowned. Her red ring? What did that mean? *Whose* red ring?

I picked up my pen and opened my notebook to a fresh page. I drew a picture of a ring—a plain band—and then another one with a large gemstone. *Her red ring. Her ring. Red ring.*

I thought about yesterday's puzzle word, TEC-PUSS. That had been an anagram for SUSPECT.

My heart skipped a beat. So maybe HER RED RING was an anagram, too.

My mind raced as I started writing down combinations of letters, one by one. There were three more letters than yesterday, making this puzzle more difficult.

I sat back and stared at the letter combinations I had written. None of them made sense. Maybe I was on the wrong track. . . .

And then the letters swam in my vision and seemed to rearrange themselves. Two words leaped out at me, clear as day.

But before I could raise my hand, Chen yelled out, "'Red herring'! The answer is 'red herring'!"

"Excellent," Ms. Darby said. "Chen Li, the blue envelope is yours." She handed it to him.

"I almost had it," Tyler grumbled in frustration.

"I know the feeling," I said sympathetically.

But Tyler wasn't listening. He got up and walked over to Chen. Althea was at Chen's side. The two of them were opening the blue envelope together.

Tyler reached into his pocket and whipped out his gold money clip. "I'll give you five hundred dollars for that clue," he said quickly. When Chen didn't reply immediately, Tyler went on. "No? Okay, I'll raise that to one thousand dollars. Take it or leave it."

"How about leave it," Chen replied drolly. "Thanks anyway, man." He touched Althea's arm, and the two of them walked off. Dee Darby gestured to one of the cameramen, who followed them.

Tyler sighed and put away his money clip. "These people don't understand basic capitalism," he complained. "If I offer you a lot of money in exchange for something that didn't you cost any money to begin with, you say yes. That's how you *make* money. It's that simple."

I peeked at my watch. It was almost eight thirty. "We should all head out," I suggested. "We have our assignments," I added, glancing meaningfully at Tyler.

Tyler nodded. "Right. The memo stands. Wendy and I will pursue Oscar Wilde, the red hair, and the 'ART' clue from yesterday. The rest of you start interviewing all the party guests."

Mary Lee opened her mouth to say something, then clamped it shut. "Fine," she said tightly.

I reached over and squeezed her arm encouragingly. I was glad she was sticking with our team—for now.

"I gathered the addresses of all the party guests this morning and marked them on a map," Hamish spoke up. "We should pay visits to Florence Pomeroy, Thierry Devereaux, Marguerite Mercier, and Sebastien Laroche first. They're the closest."

"Good work, Sherlock Holmes," Fish complimented him.

"And I have my tape recorder all ready," I said, patting my jacket pocket. "Let's go!"

Our first visit was with Mrs. Gory's friend, Florence Pomeroy. Ms. Pomeroy lived in an old townhouse on a charming street called Rue Jacob, in the sixth arrondissement.

Her maid led us into a living room that was decorated entirely in red. The walls were crammed with framed French movie posters and black-and-white photographs of cats. There were *real* cats everywhere: two on the couch, one on the floor, and three others wandering in and out of the room.

Madame Pomeroy was sitting on the couch, petting one of the cats. She stood up to greet us. She was tall and slender, with a pale, freckled complexion.

And she had red hair.

"Red hair," Hamish whispered in my ear.

"I noticed," I whispered back. I smiled at Madame Pomeroy. "Thank you for seeing us," I said, more loudly. I reached into my pocket and clicked on the tape recorder.

Madame Pomeroy stroked her cat and smiled a toothy smile. "Can I get any of you some café au lait? It's an absolutely uncivilized hour to be having a conversation *without* coffee."

"No, thank you, Madame Pomeroy," Hamish replied. "We have some questions to ask you about Sir Adrian's birthday party. You were one of the guests, right?"

"Oh, yes! Well! If you ask me, that party was doomed from the start." Madame Pomeroy narrowed her eyes ominously.

"Why do you say that, Madame Pomeroy?" Mary Lee asked her.

"My astrologer told me that morning that it would be a bad-luck day," Madame Pomeroy explained. "Something about the alignment of the

111

planets. I called Gillian and told her so. But she insisted on having the party anyway. Really, she should have listened to me!"

I scribbled some notes into my notebook, then glanced up. "What time did you arrive at the Gorys' house?"

Madame Pomeroy considered this. "Hmm. It was seven o'clock, exactly. I remember looking at my watch."

"What did you do after you arrived?" Hamish asked her.

"Gillian greeted me in the front hall. We spent a few minutes talking about our cats." Madame Pomeroy beamed at the cat on her lap. "As you can see, I'm quite fond of cats. This one here is Miaou Miaou, and the other one on the sofa is Fromage, which is French for "cheese," and the one nibbling on your shoe, Hamish, is Oscar. There are three more wandering about. They're all Siamese. Adrian and Gillian have a calico, Lulu. She's quite an unfriendly little creature. She only likes Adrian, for some reason."

Fish nodded understandingly. "I have a pet iguana back home, and he's the exact same way."

"What happened after that?" I asked Madame Pomeroy, trying to get her back on track.

"Hmm . . . Gillian interrupted me while I was in the middle of telling her about Oscar's digestive problems,"

Madame Pomeroy replied. "She said that she'd forgotten to put on her diamond necklace. She apologized and excused herself so she could go get it."

"Where did she go?" Mary Lee asked her.

Madame Pomeroy cocked her head. "Down the hallway, I believe. I went into the living room to mingle with the other guests. A few minutes later, I heard a scream from the kitchen. I didn't think anything of it. I figured the cook must have burned the soufflé again. I don't know why they don't just fire him and get a new one!"

"What were you doing when you heard the scream?" Fish spoke up.

"I was in the living room talking to my friend Marguerite Mercier," Madame Pomeroy replied.

I glanced at her hair. "By the way, I love your hair. It's the same color red as, um, a friend of mine's back home."

Madame Pomeroy beamed. "*Merci beaucoup*. All the women in my family are redheads. It explains why we all have fiery, passionate natures."

I smiled. "That's so interesting. One last thing, Madame Pomeroy. Do you own a diamond necklace?"

Madame Pomeroy shook her head. "Oh, goodness no. I only wear emeralds. Diamonds are bad luck for my birth month! That's what my astrologer says, anyway."

"As I always told Gillian, you do not keep a million-dollar diamond necklace in your house!" Thierry Devereaux said when we visited him. "You just don't! You keep it in a high-security vault with twenty-four-hour-a-day armed guards!"

Monsieur Devereaux was a short, portly man with thinning black hair and a mustache. He lived in a large, modern apartment with a view of the Eiffel Tower.

"Is there anything you can tell us about the party that might help us find the thief?" I asked him. "For example, where were you when the maid screamed?"

"I believe I was in the dining room sampling the hors d'oeuvres," Monsieur Devereaux said after a moment. "Fabulous shrimp!" he added.

"We hear you're a big fan of fancy jewels yourself, Monsieur Devereaux," Fish spoke up. "Is that true?

Monsieur Devereaux shrugged. "*Oui*, of course. The ladies, they expect that sort of thing. The salesmen at Laurier know me very well. I'm there often. I have many lady friends."

Fish beamed at Mary Lee. "Mary Lee, maybe I could take you shopping at Laurier? Would you like that?" Mary Lee blushed and continued scribbling in her notebook.

"It must get very expensive, having so many women friends," I pointed out to Monsieur Devereaux.

He shrugged again. "A man does what he has to do."

Hamish waved his pipe at him. "Sir, are you familiar with the Sherlock Holmes story 'The Adventure of the Six Napoleons'?" It involves a rather intriguing hiding place for a priceless gem. . . ."

"Hamish!" Fish, Mary Lee, and I said at the same time.

"What did Florence Pomeroy say about me?" Marguerite Mercier demanded.

Madame Mercier lived in a beautiful townhouse in the seventh arrondissement. She had silvery blond hair that was piled high on her head and piercing blue eyes. She was dressed in a purple silk dress and lots of shiny jewelry. I couldn't tell if they were real stones or not.

"She said you were in the living room talking to her when the maid screamed," Hamish replied. "Is that right?

Madame Mercier nodded slowly. "Oh. Yes. I think that's right. Yes. Or maybe I was upstairs at the time. It's one or the other." She stared at the large blue ring on her hand, as though it were a crystal ball that could tell her the answer.

"Is there anything you remember from the party that might help us find the thief?" I asked her.

Madame Mercier's eyes lit up. "Yes, absolutely!"

she said eagerly. "I can tell you who your thief is, right now!"

Mary Lee leaned forward. "Really? Who is it?"

"I saw a suspicious character hovering outside just as I arrived at the party," Madame Mercier announced dramatically.

Hamish flipped to a fresh page in his notebook. "Can you give us a description of this person?"

Madame Mercier frowned. "Well, it was rather dark."

"Was it a guy or a girl?" Fish said helpfully.

"As I said, it was rather dark," Madame Mercier replied. "It could have been a man or a woman, I'm not sure. Besides, the person was wearing some sort of hat. Or perhaps it was a hood. Or perhaps it was one of those things you Americans like to wear, those baseball caps. I don't remember, exactly."

"What makes you say that this person was acting suspiciously?" I asked her.

"I have a tremendous sixth sense about people," Madame Mercier explained. "I can just tell these things. For example, my dear . . . Nadine, right?"

"Nancy," I corrected her.

"Nancy. For example, I can tell that you grew up on a farm and always dreamed of becoming an opera singer. Am I right? I'm right, aren't I? So there, now you know what I mean about my sixth sense." Madame Mercier smiled triumphantly.

NANCY'S NOTES, TUESDAY

*Florence Pomeroy has red hair(!). Confirmed
  Mrs. Gory was talking to her in hallway, then
  excused herself to get diamond necklace.
*Madame Pomeroy said she herself was in
  living room talking to Marguerite Mercier
  when maid screamed. Madame Mercier
  couldn't remember.
*Thierry Devereaux says he was in the dining
  room all this time. Need to confirm. Likes
  ~~$ $ $~~ jewelry
*Madame Mercier thinks she saw suspicious
  figure outside of party-but fuzzy on details.

We visited eight more of the "early bird" party guests after that, accompanied the whole time by two cameramen. None of those interviews yielded any useful intel, though. All eight people were either in the living room or the dining room when the maid Josette screamed, and a few minutes later, when the necklace was stolen. They all had alibis for the entire time.

We only had one more name on the list: Sebastien Laroche. According to Mr. Gory, Monsieur Laroche was his colleague at the British Embassy as well as his best friend. Mrs. Gory told us later that he was from one of the wealthiest and most prominent families in Paris.

Monsieur Laroche lived in a townhouse just off the Place des Vosges, which was a beautiful old square in the fourth arrondissement, on the Right Bank. It was nearly three o'clock in the afternoon when Hamish, Mary Lee, Fish, and I arrived at his door. The street was filled with children in dark blue uniforms just getting out of school.

We knocked on Monsieur Laroche's door. No one answered. "Maybe he's not home," Mary Lee suggested.

I knocked again—and again. There was a small silver convertible parked in the driveway. There was a good chance *someone* was home.

After a moment, the door opened. A tall, elderly-looking man frowned at the four of us and said nothing.

"*Parlez-vous anglais?*" I said, asking him if he spoke English.

"*Oui.* Yes. What do you want?" the man asked me suspiciously.

The man was standing in a small, dimly lit hallway. Behind him, I could make out a tall potted plant, an umbrella stand, and a large mirror hanging on the wall.

"Are you Monsieur Laroche?" Hamish spoke up.

The man glanced ever so slightly over his shoulder. "No. I am the *majordome*—the butler. I am afraid

Monsieur Laroche is not home. You will have to come back another time."

The butler began to close the door. Just then, I noticed something glinting in the mirror. It was the reflection of a person—a man.

The man had red hair.

The reflection flickered away, but before the door closed completely, I heard a voice. "Who is it, Gaston?" said the voice—someone with a thick Brooklyn accent.

The door closed. I turned to Hamish, Mary Lee, and Fish. "There's someone in there," I announced excitedly. "And he has red hair. We *have* to find a way to see him!"

10

The Impostor

But, Nancy! The butler said Monsieur Laroche wasn't home," Mary Lee pointed out.

"I'm not sure if it was Monsieur Laroche. He didn't sound French," I said. "We have to find out for sure. He's a redhead! The only other redhead we've come across so far is Florence Pomeroy."

"Perhaps Tyler and Wendy have had more luck in the redhead department," Hamish said.

"I hope so. In the meantime, we need to follow this lead," I said.

"How are we going to do that?" Fish said. "The butler kind of slammed the door on us. He wasn't exactly filled with the aloha spirit."

"This reminds me of a Sherlock Holmes story," Hamish began. "The one I was telling you about this morning, Mary Lee—'A Scandal in Bohemia.' In that story, Holmes has to get inside someone's house in order to find a very important photograph. He goes to the person's door faking an injury so that the person has no choice but to let him in."

"You want me to pretend I have a broken leg or something?" Fish offered.

I was silent as I tried to figure out a plan. We could fake an injury, as Hamish had suggested. No. We could lie our way in. No. We could break in. Definitely no.

And then the answer came to me. Persistence. I would simply keep knocking until the butler let me in.

I lifted my hand and began knocking. And knocking.

Mary Lee stood close to me. "What are you doing, Nancy?" she whispered. One of the cameramen moved in, trying to capture what we were saying on tape.

"I'm going to bother the butler until he lets me in," I whispered back.

Hamish nodded. "I think Sherlock Holmes would approve of that strategy."

After a few minutes, the door burst open. The butler stood there, his face beet-red. "This is harassment, young lady," he blustered. "If you don't stop right this second, I am going to be forced to call the police."

I stared the butler straight in the eye. "We know

121

there's someone here," I said levelly. "Someone with red hair. We need to speak to him. Is he a friend of Monsieur Laroche?"

The butler gaped. He glanced over his shoulder, looking uncomfortable. "Uh . . . that is . . . um . . . ," he stammered.

"It is okay, Gaston. I will see them."

A man walked into the hallway. He was the same man I had seen in the hallway mirror a minute ago. He was short and plump, with thin red hair and nervous brown eyes. I stared at his head and thought about the fine red hair I had found in the safe.

"I am Sebastien Laroche," the man said. "What is going on, please?" The question was directed at me.

I stared at him in confusion. His voice was elegant and refined, with a touch of a French accent. But moments ago I had heard him speak with a heavy Brooklyn accent.

"You're . . . Monsieur Laroche?" I asked him.

The man narrowed his eyes at me. "*Oui, c'est moi.*"

"And *his* name is Gaston?" I said, pointing to the butler.

"*Oui,*" Monsieur Laroche replied.

I churned this over in my brain. In reality these two men were two actors playing Monsieur Laroche and Gaston the butler. Monsieur Laroche and Gaston were both supposed to be French. But the actor playing Monsieur Laroche had spoken with a Brooklyn accent a moment ago.

Had that been the actor speaking in a Brooklyn accent, or Monsieur Laroche speaking in a Brooklyn accent? I wondered. It had to be the latter, I thought, since he had called the butler "Gaston"—not "Bob" or "François" or whatever the other actor's name might be.

Something weird was going on. I decided to take a chance and confront Monsieur Laroche. "You're not really French, are you, Monsieur Laroche?" I burst out.

Monsieur Laroche turned pale. "I—that is—what are you talking about?" he blustered.

"I overheard you talking to your butler," I replied. "You sounded American."

Monsieur Laroche hesitated. Then he sighed. "Fine, I give up, you got me," he said, dropping the French accent. "You might as well come in, all of youse." He sounded like a totally different person.

"Whoa, this is weird," Fish said in a low voice as the four of us walked into the house, trailed by the two cameramen. Gaston, the butler, closed the door behind us. "Do you think he's a shape-shifter, or what?"

"Something is definitely not right," I agreed.

We followed Monsieur Laroche down the hallway, then into a large, spacious living room. There was a marble coffee table in the middle of the room, piled high with French books and magazines. The walls were covered with antique maps. Yet again, I marveled at how real all the *Mystery Solved!* sets were. The eleven other party guests we visited had equally lived-in-looking homes.

Monsieur Laroche gestured for us to sit down on the brown leather couch. "So I suppose you all wanna know my story," he said.

"All we want to know is, where is the diamond necklace?" Hamish demanded. "We found a red hair at the scene of the crime. You're a redhead. Therefore, you're our thief. Confess, sir!"

Monsieur Laroche looked confused. "That string of rocks? I had nuttin' to do wit dat."

"You didn't?" I said skeptically.

Monsieur Laroche shook his head. "Nuh-uh. The only secret I got is my, uh, what do you call it—my identity. I'm not really Sebastien Laroche. My real name is Billy Black."

"Sir," Gaston said in a warning voice. "Do you really think this is wise?"

"Billy Black?" Hamish, Mary Lee, Fish, and I said in unison. This was getting weirder and weirder—especially since none of it was real.

"Dat's me. See, I'm an ex-con from Poughkeepsie, New York. I did ten years in the big house for burglary. Dat means jail," Monsieur Laroche/Mr. Black explained. "No one in Paris knows my secret. I made up a whole new, ya know, identity." His French accent returned. "Now I'm Sebastien Laroche. Born and bred in Paris, educated at the finest universities in the world. I wanted to make a better life for myself. Can any of you blame me?"

"How we feel isn't important," I told him. "What's important is that you tell us whatever you know about the missing necklace."

Monsieur Laroche/Mr. Black shook his head. "I don't know anything. I had nothing to do with that. You must believe me."

He was still speaking in his "French" voice. I shook my head, trying to keep it all straight. An actor from who-knows-where was playing the part of an ex-con from Brooklyn who was pretending to be a wealthy, sophisticated man from Paris. This was getting confusing!

But he was the best suspect we had so far. He had red hair. He had been in prison once, for burglary.

"You have a criminal record," I pointed out. "And you have a history of lying. Your entire life is a lie."

"Perhaps. But I am not lying about this. I did not steal the necklace," Monsieur Laroche/Mr. Black insisted.

Mary Lee raised her hand. "Sir? Let's talk about

the night of Sir Adrian's birthday party. Where were you when the maid screamed?"

"I was having a conversation with the birthday boy in the living room," he said without hesitating. "Adrian was holding that horrid little cat—what is its name? Lulu. I'm allergic to cats, so I started sneezing like mad. I had to ask one of the maids—I think her name was Adele—for tissues and allergy medicine. I followed her upstairs. That's when I heard the scream." He added, "I was nowhere near the library when the necklace was stolen. If you don't believe me, just ask this maid."

"Don't worry, we will," I promised him. "And if it turns out that this is another one of your lies, we'll be back."

"There's nothing we can't get to the bottom of, Monsieur Laroche or Mr. Black or whatever your name is," Hamish warned him.

The Café Le Monde was just off the lobby of the Hotel Royale. Mary Lee, Hamish, Fish, and I sat at a table near the door, drinking coffee and snacking on pastries. One of the cameramen hovered near us, recording our conversation.

"So do you think this La Roach dude was telling the truth, Nancy?" Fish piped up.

I shrugged. "Maybe. Maybe not. We'll know for

sure as soon as we double-check his alibi with the Gorys' maid Adele."

Just then, there was a loud beeping sound. It seemed to be coming from . . . me.

"Is that your super high-tech tape recorder, Nancy?" Mary Lee asked me.

I reached into my coat pocket. It was George's PDA. "No, it's this," I replied. The mailbox icon was blinking. "I have an e-mail." Maybe George has some new news about DOOMSDAY246, I thought.

But the e-mail was not from George. It was from someone named TJCOX5. Tyler Cox?

The message read:

```
Nancy and crew,
Wendy and I just acquired this
morning's "Clue Challenge" clue from
Chen and Althea. The details of how are
unimportant. We'll share it with the
four of you if you'll agree to pay us
50% of your prize money, assuming the
six of us win. Deal?
Tyler J. Cox
```

Amused, I read Tyler's e-mail out loud to Mary Lee, Hamish, and Fish.

"What do you think?" I said when I had finished.

"No deal, y'all," Mary Lee said immediately.

"I agree with Mary Lee," Fish said. "As always."

"Who does Tyler think he is, anyway?" Hamish grumbled. "You know, he's beginning to remind me of Sherlock Holmes's extremely annoying archnemesis, Professor Moriarty."

I reread Tyler's e-mail. The six of us were supposed to be a team, as of this morning, anyway. Why didn't Tyler and Wendy just share the clue with the rest of us instead of charging us money for it? Tyler's opportunistic attitude was rearing its ugly head.

"I agree with all of you," I said finally. "No deal. If Tyler and Wendy want to form their own miniteam, let them. If they don't want to share their intel with us, we don't have to share our intel with them."

Mary Lee shook her head. "Absolutely not."

"Can you e-mail him back, Nancy?" Fish asked me.

I nodded and typed a response:

```
Hi, Tyler. Sorry, no deal. I guess
this means the team is splitting up.
Nancy, Hamish, Mary Lee, and Fish
```

I had just hit the Send button when something occurred to me.

How did Tyler get my e-mail address?

11

A Mysterious Conversation

We were on our third round of espressos and going over our notes from the day when the hotel clerk rushed into the Café Le Monde. Her name tag said YVETTE.

"Excuse me," Yvette said apologetically. "I just received a letter from Mrs. Gillian Gory, by messenger. It is addressed to 'The Detectives.' You are 'The Detectives,' no?"

"Yes," I said.

"Here you go, then." Yvette handed me a cream-colored envelope. The words "For the Detectives" and "Private and Confidential" were written on it in fancy-looking cursive letters.

"I wonder what Mrs. Gory wants from us?" Hamish said after Yvette left.

"There's only one way to find out," I said, ripping open the envelope.

Just then, Chen and Wendy walked into the café, followed by Dee Darby, Elizabeth, and Jean Alain. "Hey, it's the competition," Chen said cheerfully. "What's going on, people?"

"We just got an important letter addressed to 'The Detectives' from—" Mary Lee stopped and clamped her hand over her mouth. She looked mortified. "Oops! I shouldn't have said that," she whispered to me.

Chen and Althea exchanged a glance. "Well, I guess we got here just in time," Althea said smoothly. "Nancy, why don't you read it out loud so we can all hear what it says?"

"You said it yourself, Chen—we're the competition," Fish pointed out. "We got this letter first. There's no way we're sharing it with you."

"Fish here is correct," Hamish agreed. "Finders, keepers, as Sherlock Holmes would say. Well, maybe that's not exactly how he would put it. But you get our drift."

The café door opened again, and Tyler and Wendy walked in, followed by another cameraman. "What's all this?" Tyler said, taking in the scene. "Are the six of you forming a team to fight Wendy and me? Well, good luck, losers. We're going to win anyway." He smiled meanly.

"They just got some letter addressed to 'The Detectives,'" Althea told Tyler and Wendy. "We think they should share it with all of us. After all, we're the detectives too."

Ms. Darby was furiously gesturing for the three cameramen to get all this on tape. "Elizabeth, please stop daydreaming and hold the boom for Andreas," she hissed at her assistant producer.

Hamish sat up very straight and looked Tyler square in the eye. "Look, Tyler, my man. You made your new loyalties clear in your e-mail to Nancy. The battle lines have been drawn. You and Wendy are a team. Chen and Althea are a team. And Nancy, Mary Lee, Fish, and *I* are a team. That means that *our* team is not going to share this letter with either of your teams. Is that clear?"

Tyler reached into his pocket and pulled out his gold money clip. "I'll give you five hundred dollars if you share it with Wendy and me," he offered. "No, make that a thousand. And forget about Chen and Althea."

"Hey!" Chen complained.

I leaned over to my teammates. "Look, maybe we *should* share the message with everyone else," I whispered. "The letter wasn't specifically addressed to the four of us." I added, "Of course, we wouldn't take Tyler's money."

"We need to be tough if we're going to win," Mary Lee whispered back.

"Mary Lee's right," Fish whispered. "Think like a shark! We're never going to win if we think like tunas or minnows."

"Sherlock Holmes would never have shared his clues with his enemies," Hamish added.

I sighed. I had been outvoted. "Okay. I give up. We'll be—um, sharks, not minnows."

"That's the spirit," Hamish said, patting me on the arm. He glanced up at Tyler, Wendy, Chen, and Althea. "Sorry, gang. We're not sharing this letter for a thousand dollars or a million dollars or any amount of money."

Tyler and the others glared at us. "Have it your way," Tyler said. "Come on, Wendy."

"Well, we tried, anyway," Althea said to Chen.

Ms. Darby ran after Tyler. "Tyler! Tyler Cox! Time for a 'Candid Confession'!" she yelled.

As soon as our team was alone, Mary Lee said, "Come on, Nancy. Let's open the envelope and see what Mrs. Gory's letter says. By the way, I am so, so sorry I spilled the beans about the letter to those guys," she added apologetically.

"Don't worry about it," I told Mary Lee.

I opened the envelope. Inside was a letter written in elegant cursive. It said:

To my dear detectives,
I forgot to mention that there
are security cameras outside our
house. There are videotapes from
the night of the party. Would you
like to see them?
Sincerely,
Gillian Gory

"Score!" Fish exclaimed. "This is awesome. Those videotapes might tell us who the thief is."

"Hey, y'all? We should get these tapes right away, before Tyler, Wendy, Althea, and Chen find out about them and beat us to the punch," Mary Lee suggested.

"Mary Lee and I could go get them and bring them right back," Fish offered. "Nancy, you and Hamish could stay here and keep going over our notes from today."

"Good thinking," Hamish agreed. "If we split up like this, we'll also lessen our chances of being followed to the Gorys' house by one of the other teams. We must always be vigilant and stay on our toes," he added earnestly.

I nodded. "Sounds like a plan. Get back here as soon as you have the videotapes and meet us in my hotel room," I said to Mary Lee and Fish. "I'll have the VCR cued up and ready to go."

★ ★ ★

Hamish and I sat on the floor of my room, poring over our notes from the day. There were piles of paper all around us as well as food we'd ordered from room service: a fancy French beef stew called *boeuf bourguignon*, mashed potatoes, salad, and slices of delicious tarte tatin, or apple tart.

Hamish and I weren't alone, though. One of the cameramen was sitting in the corner of the room, recording everything. He even set the camera on a tripod and started chowing down on pizza while he worked. It was weird being videotaped while hanging out in my room, but I tried to forget that the guy was there and to "act natural."

"Okay, let's go over our suspects one more time," I said to Hamish. "There's Josette, the maid who screamed when she allegedly saw a mouse. It's possible that she and a partner conspired to steal the necklace. But the other maid, Odile, confirmed that there really was a mouse."

Hamish tapped his pen against his notebook. "Then there's Florence Pomeroy. She was in the front hall talking to Mrs. Gory when Mrs. Gory went to get her diamond necklace. She claims she didn't follow Mrs. Gory but went into the living room to talk to Marguerite Mercier. Madame Mercier confirmed this, sort of. She didn't seem like she really remembered, one way or the other. Plus, Madame Pomeroy has red hair." He glanced up from his notebook. "Hmm, I think we should move Madame Pomeroy to the top of the suspect list."

"Even though her astrologer told her that diamonds were bad luck for her birth sign?" I joked.

Hamish chuckled. "Even though."

"Then there's Thierry Devereaux, who apparently likes giving expensive jewelry to his many girlfriends," I went on. "He says he was in the dining room eating hors d'oeuvres when the theft happened. We need to confirm that with the staff."

"Then there's Sebastien Laroche, aka Billy Black," Hamish said.

I nodded. "He says he was upstairs with Adele the maid at the time of the theft, getting tissues and medicine, because Lulu the cat gave him an allergy attack," I noted. "We need to confirm that with Adele."

"I'm writing all this down," Hamish said, scribbling in his notebook.

While Hamish took notes, I thought about Mr. Black's red hair and the red hair I'd found in the safe. It was an important clue. I also thought about the *International Post* clue that had led us to *The Picture of Dorian Gray* and Père Lachaise. Had Wendy and Chen found a clue at Oscar Wilde's gravesite?

There was also the answer to the "Clue Challenge": the word "art." What did that mean? And now, Chen, Althea, Tyler, and Wendy all knew the second "Clue Challenge" clue as well. What could it be?

Finally, there was the business about "the mole." I had kept my promise to Jean Alain and not shared that information with any of my team members. I wondered who the mole was. I stared at Hamish. Could it be him? It didn't seem likely. Still . . .

Hamish's voice cut into my thoughts. "What about the suspicious character whom Madame Mercier allegedly saw outside the party? Do we believe her or do we not?"

"It's worth asking the staff," I replied, trying to refocus on the case. "Plus, if there really *was* a suspicious character outside, we might see him or her on the videotapes from the security cameras."

Hamish glanced at his watch. It wasn't a regular wristwatch but an old-fashioned pocket watch that he kept on a chain. "Speaking of which . . . where on Earth are Fish and Mary Lee?" he said, sounding troubled. "It's almost nine o'clock. They've been gone for hours. They should have been back by now."

"I know," I agreed. "It *is* late. But maybe they're following an important lead."

"Maybe," Hamish said.

"Why don't I call their rooms, just to make sure?" I suggested.

Hamish nodded. "Good idea."

It was after midnight. I was in bed, tossing and turning, unable to fall asleep.

Hamish and I had said good night just before eleven and promised to regroup in the morning. Mary Lee and Fish hadn't returned, and we hadn't heard from them, despite our calling their respective rooms and leaving them half a dozen messages. I was really starting to worry about them. Where were they? Why were they incommunicado?

I leaned over to the nightstand and checked to see if the message light was blinking on my phone. It wasn't. I also checked George's PDA to see if there might be any new e-mails. There weren't.

Sighing, I lay back down and tried to fall asleep. The events of the day were crowding my brain and clamoring for attention. This case was more complicated than I had thought—especially because there were other people muddying the waters, namely Tyler, Wendy, Chen, and Althea.

I had just dropped off to sleep when something woke me up. There were voices arguing in the hallway.

"Did you get what we needed?" It was a man's low, urgent voice. He sounded familiar.

"While she was interviewing Tyler, I stole her passkey and snuck into her room." It was a woman. She sounded familiar too. "I think I know where we need to break in next."

The voices grew softer. I sat up groggily and strained to listen. I could make out only a few words here and there: "Plan B" and "Diamonds."

Breaking in? Diamonds?

This conversation was definitely getting my attention. I got out of bed and moved across the room as quietly as possible.

I pressed my ear against the door. Silence. I peered through the peephole. I saw only a wide-angle view of the hallway, other doors, potted plants, the elevator— no people.

I opened my door and stepped outside.

There was no one there.

12

Game Over

The next morning at 7:00 a.m., I went downstairs and found Dee Darby in the Savoie Room. She was setting up for this morning's "Clue Challenge."

"I have to talk to you," I told Ms. Darby. "In private."

Ms. Darby's face lit up. "Oh, you want to do a 'Candid Confession' segment right now? Fabulous! Are you having trouble with another contestant? Tyler? Mary Lee? Hamish? Or one of the others?" She glanced around. "Jean Alain! Get over here with your camera, ASAP."

I turned to Jean Alain and shook my head. "No! No camera." I turned back to Ms. Darby and lowered my voice. "I need to talk to you about something un-related to the show. Please."

139

Ms. Darby regarded me doubtfully. "Hmm, okay," she said finally. "Five minutes. I'm very busy right now."

"Five minutes," I agreed.

We walked into one of the small rooms adjoining the Savoie Room. "So what's up?" Ms. Darby said. She glanced at her watch and then at the door, her expression impatient.

I told her about the conversation I had overheard last night. "Someone obviously broke into your room while you were interviewing Tyler yesterday," I finished. "Is everything okay? Is anything missing from your room?"

For a moment, Ms. Darby stared at me blankly. Then she burst into laughter. "I think you're blurring the lines between television and reality, Nancy," she said. "You're on this show to solve a *fake* mystery. There's no *real* mystery going on."

"But what if there are *two* mysteries going on?" I suggested. "A fake mystery *and* a real mystery? The person who broke into your room found something there—something important. She said, 'I think I know where we need to break in next.'"

"That just doesn't make any sense," Ms. Darby replied. "You said you were asleep when you woke up and overheard this so-called conversation. Is it possible that you just dreamed the whole thing?"

"I don't think so," I said.

Ms. Darby patted me on the arm. "Listen. It's easy to get caught up in things and let your imagination run wild when you're on my show. I've seen it happen to other contestants. My advice? Stay focused on your clues and suspects. Your *fake* clues and suspects. Remember, Nancy Drew," she added meaningfully. "None of this is reality."

It was five minutes after eight, time for the third "Clue Challenge" segment. All the contestants were in the Savoie Room, ready and in place. All the contestants, that is, except for Mary Lee and Fish.

"Where are Ms. Abernathy and Mr., uh, Fish?" Ms. Darby demanded. "Elizabeth! Find them, immediately!"

"Yes, Ms. Darby," Elizabeth said. She punched some numbers into her cell phone. Then she rushed off in the direction of the lobby, almost tripping on her high heels.

Hamish leaned toward me. "I must say, this is most peculiar," he whispered. "We haven't seen Mary Lee and Fish or heard from them since we parted ways at the Café Le Monde yesterday. They were supposed to get those videotapes at the Gory residence and report back to us."

"I know," I whispered back. "I hope nothing happened to them."

"I hope so too."

And then something occurred to me. The voices I had heard in the hallway last night had belonged to a man and a woman. The voices had seemed familiar. And despite what Ms. Darby had said, I didn't think I had dreamed the whole thing.

Could the voices have belonged to Mary Lee and Fish? I wondered. Could they be part of some real mystery that was related—or not related—to the fake mystery?

No way, I thought. Mary Lee and Fish? How could it be possible? They were both so . . . *nice*. Of course, their sweet personalities could be pure acting. I wasn't sure what to think anymore.

Elizabeth returned to the Savoie Room. "The hotel clerk said that they, uh, came in late last night and then left again really early this morning," she announced breathlessly to Ms. Darby. "That's all she knows."

"Well, that is just unacceptable," Ms. Darby snapped. "All of our cameramen are accounted for, which means that they are off on their own without being taped. Elizabeth, this is all your fault!"

"Yes, Ms. Darby," Elizabeth said, her cheeks flushing.

"Find them immediately. In the meantime, we need to proceed with our 'Clue Challenge' segment without them." Ms. Darby gestured to the other contestants and me. "Please sit down. Elizabeth, pass out the puzzle."

"Yes, Ms. Darby," Elizabeth said.

I sat down in one of the chairs and took out my notebook and pen. Despite everything that was going on, I had to focus on the "Clue Challenge" puzzle. When Elizabeth handed me my piece of paper, I unfolded it quickly.

This morning's puzzle was similar to the other two, from yesterday and the day before. It consisted of a single word:

DIVECEEN

I stared at the word. DIVECEEN. The other two "Clue Challenge" puzzles had been anagrams. So I figured this was an anagram too.

It also occurred to me that the answers to the other two puzzles had a mystery theme: "suspect" and "red herring." So maybe the answer to this one was mystery-related too.

I got out my pen and notebook and began rearranging letters. *EN. EC. ED. EV.*

It only took me a minute to get the answer.

"'Evidence.' It's 'evidence'!" I shouted without raising my hand. I didn't want Chen or anyone else to beat me to the punch, like yesterday.

"Correct answer, Nancy," Ms. Darby said. "Today's clue is yours." She handed me a blue envelope.

I opened it quickly, with Hamish looking over my shoulder. I angled the blue card away from Chen, Althea, Tyler, and Wendy so they couldn't see it.

On the blue card was a single word: OR.

I frowned. Or? What did that mean?

I glanced briefly at Chen. I realized that I probably needed the clue he had won during yesterday's "Clue Challenge." With that clue, and with the "ART" clue, maybe today's clue would make sense.

As if reading my mind, Chen said, "Nancy. I'll show you my clue from yesterday if you'll show me yours."

"Unacceptable," Tyler spoke up at once. "I paid you a lot of money for that clue, Chen. You can't just show it to Nancy for free."

So that's how Tyler and Wendy got yesterday's clue, I thought. Taylor bought it.

"It wouldn't be for free, o brilliant one," Althea pointed out to Tyler. "It would be in exchange for clue number three."

Tyler elbowed Chen aside and marched up to me. "In that case, Nancy, trade with me. I'll give you yesterday's clue in exchange for today's clue. Leave Chen and Althea out of the deal. In fact, we can all team up again: you, Hamish, Wendy, and me—and Mary Lee and Fish, too, if they ever turn up."

I turned to Hamish. This wasn't my decision alone. "What should we do?" I whispered to him.

"I have no idea," Hamish whispered back. "We're going to have to choose between the Chen-Althea team and the Tyler-Wendy team. It's an important strategic matter. Why don't we give this some careful thought and decide, say, later this morning?"

I nodded. "Good plan," I whispered.

I turned to the other contestants and announced my decision to them. Tyler, Wendy, Chen, and Althea did not look happy.

Just then, Ms. Darby marched up to Chen, followed by one of the cameramen. "I need you for a 'Candid Confession' segment, in the other room, Chen," she said cheerfully. "Now, please."

"Whatever," Chen said, scowling at me.

I took a deep breath. Ms. Darby was no doubt going to bait Chen into saying lots of nasty things about a certain person: me.

After leaving the hotel, Hamish and I headed for the Gorys' house, followed by Jean Alain. Mrs. Gory answered the door.

"Detectives!" she cried out as soon as she saw us.

I frowned, confused. Mrs. Gory was not speaking with her usual British accent. She was speaking with a Southern drawl, like Mary Lee.

"I'm so relieved you're here," Mrs. Gory went on. "Something is very wrong."

"What do you mean, uh, Mrs. Gory—or whoever you are?" Hamish asked her. He was just as confused as I was about why "Mrs. Gory" was slipping out of character.

"You can call me Vera for the moment. That's the name I go by as an actor." Vera glanced at Jean Alain. "Turn that off, please. We're off-camera now."

"But Ms. Darby says we have to keep the camera on at all times," Jean Alain protested.

"I don't care what Ms. Darby says. Turn that off. This isn't part of the mystery," Vera insisted.

Jean Alain glanced at me and shrugged, as if to say, *What am I supposed to do?* Then he clicked the camera off.

"What's going on?" I asked Vera curiously.

Vera gestured for Hamish and me to come inside. She led us into the living room. "Someone tried to break into this house last night," she said in a low, agitated voice.

"What?" I said, shocked. "How do you know? Was anything taken? Are you guys okay?"

"Trevor—that's the actor who plays Sir Adrian— and I sleep here every night, in the upstairs bedrooms," Vera explained. "It's part of making our lives as Sir Adrian and Mrs. Gory seem 'real'—especially since you detectives and your camera crew could show up in the middle of the night, for all we know. Anyway, last night, around four a.m., I heard a noise downstairs. I thought it was the dog or the cat. I came down, to make sure."

"What happened?" Hamish prompted her.

"I saw two shadowy figures outside the living room window," Vera went on. "It seemed like one of them was about to pry the window open with some sort of tool. When I turned the living room light on, they ran."

"That's terrible!" Hamish exclaimed.

"Trevor came downstairs a few minutes later," Vera went on. "When I told him what happened, he got a flashlight and went outside. But there was no one there."

"Did you call the police?" I asked her.

Vera shook her head. "I didn't know what to do. I called Ms. Darby at the hotel and woke her up. She said it was probably some kids pulling a prank. She doesn't want the *real* police brought in because she's afraid it will interfere with the show. But I don't know," she said, frowning unhappily. "Maybe it's not safe for Trevor and the other actors and me to stay here anymore."

I churned over this latest turn of events in my mind. I had overheard the man and the woman in the hotel hallway last night, taking about a break-in.

Then two people had tried to break into the Gorys' townhouse. These incidents *had* to be related.

But what had the mystery pair been after? What had they found in Ms. Darby's hotel room that had led them to the Gorys' townhouse? Was it something connected to the Laurier diamond necklace? Or something else altogether?

Then I remembered Mary Lee and Fish.

"Did Mary Lee Abernathy and Fish come by here yesterday?" I asked Vera. "You know, the woman with the curly blond hair and the surfer guy?"

Vera nodded. "Oh, yes, they were here. They asked to see the security videotapes. They left with them."

"Do you know what was on those videotapes?" I asked her.

Vera shook her head. "No. Those are clues for the *Mystery Solved!* mystery. You detectives are the only ones who would be interested in what's on them."

I nodded, considering this. So Mary Lee and Fish had come by for the videotapes. But where were they now? Why had they gone AWOL?

A disturbing thought occurred to me. Could *they* have tried to break into the Gorys' townhouse at 4:00 a.m.?

"Do you have a real security system, or were those videotapes from a fake security system?" I asked her.

I was having a hard time keeping track of what was real and what was fake.

"We do not have a real security system, as far as I know," Vera replied. "Those videotapes I gave Mary Lee and Fish were created by the show as clues."

Just then, something began beeping. It was George's PDA.

I pulled it out of my pocket. I had a new message. "Excuse me," I said to Vera and Hamish.

I walked into the hallway, so I could have some privacy. I pressed some buttons.

My heart skipped a beat. The new message was from DOOMSDAY246.

It said:

```
You're in danger, Nancy Drew.
Back off before it's too late. Or else.
```

I stared at the words on the tiny screen. A chill ran down my spine. DOOMSDAY246's messages were getting more intense. First they warn me to get ready for a "bumpy ride." Then to "trust no one."

Now, DOOMSDAY246 was clearly threatening me.

I reread the message. Back off from what, I wondered. The fake mystery—or the real mystery?

Because more and more, I was beginning to think there were *two* mysteries. The missing Laurier diamond necklace was the fake mystery. The voices in the hallway and the attempted break-in had to do with a real mystery.

Were the two mysteries connected? They *had* to be. But how?

Jean Alain popped his head into the hallway. "Everything okay, Nancy?" he asked me worriedly.

I slipped George's PDA back into my pocket. "I'm fine," I said quickly.

He walked over to me. "I have some new information for you," he said in a low voice.

I raised my eyebrows. "What?"

"Remember the mole I mentioned to you?" Jean Alain said. I nodded. "I think it might be Mary Lee or Fish."

"Why?" I asked him curiously.

"I overheard Darby saying some stuff about them. I'm not one hundred percent positive, but I'm working on getting more info for you. I'm keeping my eyes and ears open for you," Jean Alain said, squeezing my arm.

"Thanks," I said.

I tried to picture Mary Lee or Fish as a spy. It was weird. Still, this entire show was all about fake versus real, about people pretending to be something they weren't. The mole business was no different.

"Oh, and I have one other thing for you," Jean

Alain added. "The clue Chen won in yesterday's 'Clue Challenge'? It's the word 'pit.' *P-i-t*. Chen and Althea were talking about it yesterday."

"Jean Alain," I said in a low voice, "you shouldn't be telling me this."

"I know, but I just did," Jean Alain said with a grin. "It's like I told you the other day, Nancy. I like you, and I want to see you win. And with all this strange stuff going on, you deserve a little extra help from your friends."

Hamish and I decided to spend the next hour interviewing the Gorys' staff, trying to confirm alibis and tie up various loose ends.

I was going to focus on the fake mystery for the moment; I didn't want to tell Hamish about the real mystery just yet. I also didn't tell Hamish about the "PIT" clue. I would figure out what to do about that later. I still felt guilty about Jean Alain feeding me inside info, but I knew without a doubt that if I told on him that Dee Darby would fire him and probably kick me off the show. River Heights Relief was counting on me!

For the moment, I turned my attention to the three maids who had joined us at the dining-room table: Gabrielle, Brigitte, and Adele.

"We're interested in the very specific window of

time during which the theft took place," I explained to the three women. "Gabrielle, you were in the living room during that time. Right?"

"*Oui*, mademoiselle," Gabrielle replied.

Jean Alain moved in with his camera, to get a close-up of Gabrielle. Seeing him, I was reminded of our conversation in the hallway just minutes ago. I wish he hadn't given me Chen's clue from yesterday's "Clue Challenge." It felt like an unfair advantage.

On the other hand, now that I had the clue, I couldn't just erase it from my brain. PIT. The three "Clue Challenge" clues were ART, OR, and PIT. Was that some sort of weird phrase: "Art or pit?" What did that mean?

"Do you remember seeing Florence Pomeroy talking to Marguerite Mercier?" Hamish was asking Gabrielle.

Gabrielle nodded. "*Oui.* They were talking about astrology, fashion, the opera—things like that."

I turned to Brigitte. "You were in the dining room during this time, right? Did you happen to see Thierry Devereaux there? He said"—I glanced down at my notes—"that he was in here for a while, sampling hors d'oeuvres."

"More like hoarding and devouring," Brigitte said, making a face. "He ate the shrimp plate and half the cheese platter by himself! Such terrible manners!"

Brigitte turned to Adele and Gabrielle and said something in rapid French. The three women broke out laughing.

Hamish wrote something down in his notebook. "Adele. Sebastien Laroche said that he asked you to get him some allergy medicine and tissues."

"*Oui,*" Adele said. "Monsieur Laroche had a terrible allergy attack because of Lulu. Monsieur Adrian's cat," she added. "I took him upstairs and found him what he needed in the master bathroom."

"Madame Mercier mentioned that she saw a suspicious figure outside just as the party started," I said to all three maids. "Did any of you see anyone like that?"

Adele, Gabrielle, and Brigitte exchanged glances.

"No," Adele said.

"Me, neither," Gabrielle added.

"Madame Mercier has been known to . . . how do you say it? Make up stories," Brigitte said. The three women broke into more laughter.

I started to say something to Hamish, then I heard the doorbell ringing—followed by loud, persistent knocking. Brigitte hurried to answer it.

I heard voices, and then footsteps, and then Elizabeth came rushing into the dining room, wobbling precariously on her high heels. Her cheeks were flushed, and she was out of breath.

"Nancy, Hamish, you need to come with me," Elizabeth panted. "We have to go join the others ASAP. And when Ms. Darby says ASAP, she means ASAP."

Jean Alain set his camera down. "What's going on, Elizabeth?" he demanded.

Elizabeth gave him a strange look. I wondered what that was about. But more than that, I wondered why Ms. Darby had summoned Hamish and me.

Mrs. Gory and Sir Adrian appeared in the doorway. "What's happening? What's all this racket?" Sir Adrian demanded.

"Yes, what's going on?" Mrs. Gory said anxiously. She was no longer Vera but back in character as Mrs. Gory.

Elizabeth turned to the couple. "Sir Adrian, Mrs. Gory, I have wonderful news. Chen Li and Althea Eisner have just found the diamond necklace!" she announced.

13

Wild Oscar's

Wild Oscar's was a pawnshop on a narrow, meandering side street near Père Lachaise that was lined with lots of funky little stores. When our taxicab pulled up in front of it, I could see through the window that everyone had already gathered inside: Dee Darby, Chen, Althea, Tyler, Wendy, and assorted crew members. Mary Lee and Fish were also there. I wondered where they had been all this time. Leo Laurier from Laurier Jewelers was there as well, dressed in a dashing gray suit.

Flashbulbs popped brightly. There was clapping and cheering. Wow, this is it, I thought. The mystery is over. The fake mystery, anyway.

"Here we go," Elizabeth said, opening the cab door for Hamish and me. "This is the big moment.

Sir Adrian and Mrs. Gory should be here in a few minutes. Jean Alain, can I talk to you for a sec?" she called out to the cameraman, who was hauling his camera out of the trunk.

"I need to get inside, Elizabeth," Jean Alain replied tersely.

"It's important, Jean Alain," Elizabeth hissed at him.

Jean Alain frowned. "Fine. Just make it quick."

I wondered if everything was okay with Elizabeth. But I didn't have time to worry about it now. I was more interested in learning how Chen and Wendy had found the diamond necklace.

"You two go on in," Elizabeth called out to Hamish and me. "I'm sorry you didn't win. Maybe another time!"

"I'm still reeling with disbelief," Hamish whispered to me as we walked into the store. "How could Chen and Wendy have found the necklace so quickly? This is only day three!"

"We're about to find out," I whispered back.

Chen and Althea stood in front of a long glass case filled with jewelry and old coins. Ms. Darby stood next to them, her perfect TV smile plastered on her face for the cameras.

Wendy and Tyler were standing together, glaring at Chen and Althea. They definitely did not look happy. Mary Lee and Fish were standing together on the other side of the room. Mary Lee glanced quickly at me. I saw a strange expression flash in her eyes. Fear. Why was she afraid of me? I wondered curiously.

"—and so Li and I realized that Oscar Wilde was *the* most important clue to this mystery," Althea was saying into Ms. Darby's microphone. "Our careful and persistent investigative work led us right here to Wild Oscar's pawnshop. This shop is owned by Mr. Zacharias, who is originally from New York City and is a huge fan of Oscar Wilde's work." She pointed to a gray-haired man who was standing behind the glass case. Mr. Zacharias smiled and waved at the cameras.

"Eisner and I knew we'd found the necklace the second we saw it," Chen went on.

"It was perfect teamwork," Althea said, grinning at her partner.

"Well, don't make us wait, Althea and Chen," Ms. Darby said. "Althea, why don't you hold up the necklace for all of us to see? Leo Laurier and I have just deactivated the security device with our remotes, so the necklace should be safe to touch." She held up her remote, as if to demonstrate. Mr. Laurier did the same.

"I'd be happy to." Althea reached into the glass case and pulled out a small blue velvet box.

The cameramen moved in closer. Jean Alain and Elizabeth walked into the shop just then. Jean Alain hoisted his camera onto his shoulder and rushed up to where Althea stood.

"In the final edit, we'll add a drumroll here," Ms. Darby called out with a grin. Everyone laughed.

Althea opened the blue velvet box. She pulled out a beautiful diamond necklace. Everyone gaped at it in awestruck silence as it twisted in the air, glittering brilliantly in the camera lights.

I moved forward and stared at the exquisite necklace . . . and stared . . .

. . . and realized that something was very, very wrong.

I pulled the photograph of the diamond necklace out of my bag and studied it. I stared at the necklace again.

"That's not Mrs. Gory's necklace," I announced. "It's a fake!"

Chen whirled on me. "How dare you, Nancy! Talk about being a bad loser!" he snapped.

Althea patted his arm. "It's okay, Li. Nothing can spoil our big moment," she reassured him.

I shook my head. "No, I meant what I said. This is a fake. Look at the clasp," I said, pointing. "It's smooth and plain. In the photograph, it has a subtle design etched into it. And check out this diamond, here." I indicated one of the larger diamonds that hung near the bottom. "It has a tiny, tiny chip. Diamonds don't chip. Otherwise, the necklace is identical to the one in the photograph. Someone obviously went to a lot of trouble to duplicate the original."

The room erupted in gasps of disbelief. Ms. Darby took the necklace from Althea and squinted at it. Then she turned to Mr. Laurier. "Leo Laurier from Laurier Jewelers, could we get your opinion?" she asked him.

Mr. Laurier stepped forward and stared at the necklace. "This is definitely a fake," he announced after a moment. "This is not the real Contessa, which is Laurier Jewelers' signature necklace. The Contessa is still out there."

The entire room fell silent. Then everyone began talking at once: "This is totally crazy—" "Where's the real necklace, then?" "Did the show set this up?" "I can't believe this happened." "What do we do now?"

Ms. Darby gestured to Althea and Chen, both of whom looked angry and embarrassed. "Althea, Chen, this is truly a shocking moment," she said to them. "I need you both for a 'Candid Confessions' segment, ASAP. Let's head outside, shall we?"

Hamish leaned toward me. "Excellent sleuthing, Nancy! This means we're still in the game!" he whispered.

"We sure are," I whispered back. "Let's get to work. But first, I want to talk to Mary Lee. I think something's bothering her."

But when I turned to look for Mary Lee, she was gone.

So was Fish.

With Mary Lee and Fish missing in action, Hamish and I were on our own. We decided to split up for the rest of the day and pursue different clues, to be efficient.

As I walked out of Wild Oscar's, I ran into Dee Darby and spotted Chen and Althea heading down the street; they had apparently just finished their "Candid Confessions" segments.

Ms. Darby was talking on her cell phone and giving orders to Elizabeth at the same time. On an impulse, I decided to ask her a few questions.

I caught her eye as she was wrapping up her call. "Yes, Nancy Drew?" she said quickly. "What can I do for you?"

"I need to talk to you for a second," I replied. "In private."

Ms. Darby raised her eyebrows at me. "Fine. Over here," she said. She gestured to a quiet spot on the sidewalk away from the rest of her crew.

When we were alone, I said, "I really think there's something going on. Something besides the *Mystery Solved!* mystery, I mean."

Ms. Darby sighed. "Yes, yes, I know. The conversation you think you heard in the hotel hallway. Really,

Nancy, that could have been anything. A practical joke by the other contestants. An elaborate night-mare. I don't exactly have the time to—"

"And then there was the attempted break-in at the townhouse," I interrupted.

"Yes, yes. Mrs. Gory—Vera—told me about that," Ms. Darby said. "Again, I don't have the time to respond to every little thing one of my contestants or actors or crew members think they saw or heard. I have a show to produce." She glanced impatiently at her watch. "Now I really must get back to work."

I could see that I was getting nowhere with Ms. Darby. I was about to thank her for her time and say good-bye when something occurred to me.

Maybe it was time to confront her about the mole.

"Can I ask you something, Ms. Darby?" I said casually. I didn't want to let on what Jean Alain had told me. I was hoping that I could provoke a reveal-ing reaction out of her, though. "I don't want to name any names. But one of the contestants doesn't seem like a real contestant. The person seems like a mole. Why would your show do a thing like that?"

Ms. Darby's face was a total blank. "A mole?" she said after a moment. "You think one of our contestants might be a mole?" She burst out laughing. "Oh, you mean like they do on that horrible reality show on a certain competing network I won't mention. You must be joking. *Mystery Solved!* doesn't resort to cheap tricks like that. We pull the highest ratings in prime-time television. Why would we spoil a successful formula?"

I watched Ms. Darby carefully. She seemed to be telling the truth—unless she was a really, really good actress. Her eyes looked totally sincere.

So maybe there was no mole.

But why would Jean Alain have told me that there *was*?

14

Picture-Perfect

I **decided that I** needed a change of scenery to mull over the case. I headed over to one of the greatest art museums in the world: the Musée du Louvre, or the Louvre Museum.

The Louvre was a magnificent palatial structure, built mostly in the sixteenth century. Parts of the foundation of the original Louvre, dating from the twelfth century, still existed. In 1989, a modern glass pyramid was added to the central courtyard. Many Parisians either loved or hated the pyramid, which was in vivid contrast to the rest of the historic structure.

Once in the vast, crowded lobby, I bought a ticket and wandered randomly down one of the long halls. I was vaguely aware of one of the cameramen— I thought his name was Andreas—following me.

I needed to think.

I passed dozens of exquisite paintings and sculptures that were hundreds of years old. I saw the famous painting of the Mona Lisa by Leonardo da Vinci. I passed paintings of Greek gods and goddesses. I passed paintings of gruesome battle scenes. I passed dozens of portraits of beautiful women in exquisite dresses and wealthy-looking men in velvet coats.

One portrait in particular caught my eye, of a woman wearing a jeweled necklace. I stopped and studied it, hoping for inspiration. Who had stolen Mrs. Gory's diamond necklace? Where was it now?

I sat down on a bench. My brain was churning with thoughts, clues, suspects. I had to organize it all.

I got my notebook and pen out and started scribbling. First, there was the fake mystery: the missing Laurier diamond necklace. There were five clues: the Dorian Gray/Oscar Wilde clue; the red hair; and the three "Clue Challenge" clues, "ART," "OR," and "PIT."

As for suspects, the strongest one was Sebastian Laroche, aka Billy Black. He was an ex-con with a burglary record and a habit of lying. He also had red hair.

Then there was what appeared to be the *real* mystery. I had overheard a strange conversation in the hall last night between a man and a woman.

They had mentioned sneaking into Ms. Darby's room as well as their plans to break in somewhere else. Then Vera—Mrs. Gory—had reported seeing two people trying to break into the townhouse in the middle of the night.

And on top of all that, Mary Lee and Fish were acting really, really bizarrely. Could one of them be the mole Jean Alain had told me about? If there even *was* a mole? This was now in doubt because of my conversation with Ms. Darby outside of Wild Oscar's.

Or were Mary Lee and Fish acting bizarrely for some other reason altogether? Could they be tied up with the real mystery somehow? Were they the couple I heard talking in the hallway?

And, of course, there were the e-mails from DOOMSDAY246 . . .

A group of schoolchildren passed by me just then, sketchbooks tucked under their arms. A stern-looking guard walked by, he said something to the cameraman in French, took a look at his permit to film, and then went on.

I stared at my notes. I had a nagging feeling that I was missing something really, really important. . . .

"Focus on the clues," I reminded myself. "It always comes down to the clues."

I flipped through my notebook slowly, running my fingers down each page. I had written the word

"Enigma" on one page and underlined it three times. That word, in the fake *International Post* article, had led to *The Picture of Dorian Gray*, Père Lachaise, and the grave of Oscar Wilde.

I glanced up from the notebook and found myself looking at a portrait of a Spanish nobleman with intelligent brown eyes. Oscar Wilde's novel, too, was about a portrait: a portrait of the main character, Dorian Gray.

It occurred to me just then that the "authors" of this mystery—the *Mystery Solved!* mystery—had gone to a lot of trouble to point to *The Picture of Dorian Gray* and Oscar Wilde. Was it so that we—the contestants—would be fooled into pursuing a red herring, namely, a fake necklace planted in Wild Oscar's pawnshop?

Or was there another reason altogether?

Codes, I thought suddenly. Maybe this all has to do with codes.

I pulled the *International Post* article out of my bag and read it once. Then twice.

I had decoded the first letter of each sentence to get "Dorian Gray."

Could "Dorian Gray" be a secondary code for something else?

Trying to stifle my excitement, I took out a pen and began scribbling words, letters, into my notebook. I applied all the various code-breaking strategies I'd used before, but nothing worked. I paused to think for a second, chewing on the end of my pen . . .

Maybe "Dorian Gray" was an anagram. I took the letters D, O, R, I, A, N, G, R, A, and Y and moved them around to form different arrangements.

Just then, a shadow fell over my notebook. The cameraman was zooming in on my scribbles. "What are you doing?" he asked me curiously.

"Trying to solve the mystery," I replied.

A, D, R . . .

I stopped writing and gasped in surprise.

"Dorian Gray" was an anagram for "Adrian Gory."

Outside the Louvre, I frantically hailed a cab.

"Hôtel Royale, *s'il vous plaît*," I said breathlessly, sliding in the backseat of the cab. The cameraman slid into the seat beside me.

"*Oui*, mademoiselle," the cab driver replied.

As the cab sped over the bridge, I barely noticed the lovely scenery: the Seine River and the beautifully gothic Notre Dame Cathedral on the Isle de la Cité, in the distance. My mind was racing with the new realization that Adrian Gory might be . . . could be . . . *was* . . . the thief.

But how was this possible?

I thought about something Sebastian Laroche, aka Billy Black, had said about the night of the party: that

Sir Adrian had been holding his calico cat Lulu while the two men talked in the living room. That's what had led to Mr. Black's allergy attack.

Lulu was a calico, with white, orange, and black fur. No doubt Sir Adrian had gotten some of Lulu's fur on his hands and clothes. Maybe the fine red hair in the safe had been Lulu's, inadvertently left there by Sir Adrian when he took his wife's necklace.

Also, Mr. Black couldn't provide an alibi for Sir Adrian between the time Josette screamed and the time the necklace disappeared. He had been upstairs with Adele, getting allergy medicine and tissues.

There was just one thing that didn't make sense: motive. Why would Sir Adrian steal his wife's necklace?

I stifled a smile. I was getting as caught up in this fake mystery as I would a real one. Now that I was close to the finish line, so to speak, I was pretty psyched.

When the cab pulled up in front of the Gorys' townhouse on Rue de Grenelle, I spotted Hamish standing outside the door. He looked as though he was about to knock.

"Hamish!" I yelled as I got out of the cab.

Hamish turned and waved at me. "Nancy! Glad to see you! Listen, I tried to find Mary Lee and Fish to ask them about the security videotapes. But alas, my mission was unfruitful. I was thinking that I might—"

"Never mind," I interrupted him. "I may have solved the mystery! Come on, I'll fill you in."

They were all inside the townhouse: Sir Adrian and Mrs. Gory, Dee Darby, Elizabeth, Jean Alain, and the six other contestants. It turned out that Tyler had convinced Wendy, Chen, Althea, Mary Lee, and Fish to form a superteam, to compete against Hamish and me. The six of them had been searching one of the maid's rooms for the necklace when Hamish and I walked through the front door. I had told Hamish everything about the "Dorian Gray" anagram and the red hair. I had also told him about the three "Clue Challenge" clues, although they still didn't make any sense to me.

Ms. Darby and Elizabeth were in the living room, going over some notes. "Hamish and I may have solved the mystery," I announced excitedly to them.

Ms. Darby jumped up from her chair. "This is fabulous news! Tell us everything! Oh, I need to call Leo Laurier and get him over here ASAP." She pulled her cell phone out of her pocket.

"Where's Sir Adrian?" Hamish asked Ms. Darby.

"He and Mrs. Gory are in the library," Elizabeth offered.

Hamish and I rushed to the library. I was aware of voices, noises behind us; I'm sure Ms. Darby and her crew were hot on our heels, although I didn't bother to turn around and look. I was too eager to get to the bottom of the mystery.

I felt a hand on my arm. I turned around. It was Jean Alain.

"So you really found it, Nancy?" he whispered, his eyes shining with excitement. "Where is it? You can tell me. We're friends."

"Not now, Jean Alain," I said.

Sir Adrian and his wife were in the library, drinking tea out of small white cups. There was a fire crackling in the fireplace.

"Why, what's all this?" Sir Adrian demanded.

"Adrian, darling, don't be rude. Would you join us for a cup of tea?" Mrs. Gory said pleasantly.

"No, thank you, Mrs. Gory," I said. I fixed my eyes on her husband. "Sir Adrian, where were you at the time of the theft?"

Sir Adrian looked startled. "What? I believe we already went over this. I was in the living room talking to my good friend Sebastien Laroche."

"What about when the maid screamed?" I persisted.

Sir Adrian crossed his long legs. "Sebastien and I continued to talk. I didn't think anything of the scream. I figured it was one of the maids getting hysterical about some silly little thing."

Hamish and I exchanged a glance. Sir Adrian had just told a lie. We knew for a fact that Sebastien Laroche, aka Billy Black, had left Sir Adrian alone then.

"You're the thief," I said, pointing to Sir Adrian. "You stole your wife's necklace!"

Sir Adrian's face turned beet-red. "That's absurd," he blustered. "Why would I steal my own wife's necklace? And if I *am* the thief, where is the necklace? This whole thing is nonsense. Come on, Gillian . . ." He stood up and made a move to leave the library.

Just then, Hamish turned to me and tugged on my sleeve. "Nancy," he whispered excitedly. "I believe I've deduced the location of the necklace!"

15

Take Two

Hamish pointed to the portrait of Sir Adrian that was hanging over the mantle. "There," he whispered to me. "That's where it is."

"What?" I whispered back. "Why do you think that?"

"I just figured out the three 'Clue Challenge' clues," Hamish replied. "'ART,' 'OR,' and 'PIT.' Those letters are an anagram for the word 'portrait.' I think the necklace is hidden in the portrait of Dorian Gray . . . I mean, Adrian Gory."

I smiled. "Brilliant deduction, Watson!"

Hamish and I hurried over to the portrait and unhooked it from the wall. By now, everyone was in the library: Dee Darby, Elizabeth, various cameramen and crew members, and the six other contestants. Mr. Laurier had arrived as well. Ms. Darby informed

Hamish and me that both she and Mr. Laurier had just deactivated the security system attached to the diamond necklace.

"What is going on?" Tyler demanded. "What are you and Hamish doing, Nancy?"

"You'll see," Hamish replied mysteriously.

"It's so unfair," Wendy muttered under her breath. "*We* were supposed to win, Tyler!"

"They haven't won yet," Chen pointed out.

Hamish and I set the portrait down on Sir Adrian's desk and turned it over carefully. The back of the painting was lined with dark brown cloth.

There was a slit in the cloth, at the bottom. Just then, I remembered seeing Sir Adrian's letter opener lying on the floor, on Monday, when we had all visited the townhouse for the first time. Sir Adrian had said something about opening his mail with it. But perhaps he had used it to cut this slit in the cloth. . . .

"There," I said, pointing to the slit.

Hamish reached inside the slit and wriggled his fingers around. "I think I feel something in there," he said eagerly.

"Jean Alain, zoom in on this!" Ms. Darby ordered, her voice rising with excitement. Jean Alain complied.

After a moment, Hamish pulled his hand out of the slit.

He was holding a diamond necklace.

The diamond necklace. It had the correct clasp, and no chips whatsoever.

The room erupted in gasps of surprise. "And we have our winners!" Ms. Darby exclaimed.

Mrs. Gory clutched her silver poodle to her chest and sank heavily into a chair. "Oh, Adrian, how could you?" she moaned. Pomme Frite began barking at Sir Adrian.

"Why did you do it, Sir Adrian?" I asked him.

Sir Adrian covered his face with his hands. "I'm so ashamed," he said finally. "Darling, I couldn't bring myself to tell you. But I've been suffering from terrible money problems. Gambling and all that, you know. So I came up with the idea of selling your necklace to pay off my debts. I knew you wouldn't part with it willingly. So I figured I would stage a 'theft' and sell the necklace on the black market, for cash. That way, you could collect the insurance money and buy yourself a new one."

"How could you, Adrian?" Mrs. Gory repeated. The poodle made a move to bite Sir Adrian. "No, Boo-Boo, no," she ordered her dog. "Violence is not the answer."

"I brainstormed all sorts of ways to stage the theft," Sir Adrian went on, facing the cameras now. "Then, the night of the party, the opportunity fell into my lap. I was in the living room when I heard Josette scream. I went to investigate. I saw Gillian running out of the library and down the hall ahead of me, toward the kitchen. As I passed the library doorway, I glanced inside and noticed that the safe was open. This was my chance! I went to the safe, took the necklace, and quickly hid it in a place no one would think to look: inside the lining of my portrait, which I quickly ripped open with a letter opener."

"Very diabolical, Sir Adrian," Ms. Darby remarked.

"I had been planning to retrieve the necklace as soon as I found a buyer," Sir Adrian finished. "I figured that, in the meantime, you detectives would finger one of the dozen party guests or one of the maids for the crime."

Mrs. Gory flung her hand against her forehead, leaned back in her chair, and fainted. Or rather, pretended to faint. The poodle began licking her face. Mrs. Gory—Vera—sure was a good actress.

Ms. Darby stood up and threw her arms around Hamish's and my shoulders. "Mystery solved!" she announced. "We have our winners!"

Flashbulbs went off, and various people clapped and cheered. I smiled dizzily at Hamish. We had done it!

"Sherlock Holmes would be proud of us," Hamish called out to me over the din and chaos in the room.

"Definitely," I agreed.

I was standing in the front hallway of the Gorys' townhouse, getting ready to go back to the hotel, when something occurred to me.

"Ms. Darby?" I called out.

Dee Darby snapped her cell phone shut and slipped into her coat. "Yes, Nancy? We have to get back to the hotel right away, you know. I need to do an up-close-and-personal interview with you and Hamish, and there's the wrap party later. Which reminds me—" She was talking a mile a minute, as usual.

"I know, I know," I interrupted her. "Something's been bugging me, though. Earlier today, I asked you whether or not one of the contestants was a mole. You said no. Is that true?"

Ms. Darby chuckled. "I meant what I said before, Nancy. None of you is a mole. We do not use moles. I don't know where you got such a crazy idea." She paused. "Although on second thought, maybe it's *not* such a crazy idea. It's good to embrace change. Elizabeth, make a note to consider using a mole in one of the future episodes. Elizabeth? Elizabeth, where are you? Elizabettthhhhh!" she yelled at the top of her lungs.

Now I was really confused. Ms. Darby had just confirmed—double-confirmed—that none of the contestants was a mole.

Jean Alain had definitely lied to me. But why?

On a hunch, I picked up my coat and bag and headed back down the hall, to the library. Jean Alain was there, closing up his camera case. Elizabeth was there too. The two of them were talking in low voices.

Low voices that sounded familiar . . . like the voices I had overheard in the hotel hallway.

They jumped in surprise when I walked into the room.

"Hey, Nancy," Jean Alain called out. He sounded uncomfortable.

Elizabeth was holding the silver box containing the diamond necklace. "We're packing things up," she said with a nervous smile. "The Boss Lady will kill me if anything happens to this," she added, indicating the box.

I fixed my eyes on Jean Alain. "There was no mole," I said pointedly. "I just double-checked with Ms. Darby, now that the mystery is solved. There was no mole. There never was a mole. So why did you tell me there was one?"

"I don't know what you're talking about, N-Nancy," Jean Alain stammered.

"Maybe you told me about the mole because you wanted to distract me," I guessed. "Maybe you were trying to make me think that you were my friend, and that I could trust you. Maybe that's why you told me about the second 'Clue Challenge' clue."

Jean Alain forced a smile. "I *am* your friend, Nancy."

"Elizabeth snuck into Ms. Darby's room using her passkey," I went on. "Something she found there told her that the Laurier necklace was hidden here, in the

Gorys' townhouse. That's why the two of you tried to break in last night. You wanted to look for it yourselves, while everyone was asleep."

"You're wrong," Jean Alain protested.

I noticed that Elizabeth was trying to leave the room. "Stop," I ordered her. "I want you to open the silver box. Now."

"No way," Elizabeth said immediately. "The Boss Lady will kill me, and—"

I dropped my coat and bag, reached over, and grabbed the silver box from Elizabeth. She and Jean Alain both lunged toward me.

I stepped back, out of their reach, and quickly opened the box.

Inside was the diamond necklace. The *fake* diamond necklace, from Wild Oscar's pawnshop.

"All right, where's the real one?" I demanded.

"Yes, Elizabeth, where's the real one? You, too, Jean Alain. You *snakes*!"

I turned around. Dee Darby was standing there, her face flushed with anger. Behind her was one of the cameramen. His camera had been taping the whole time.

Just then, I noticed that Jean Alain was holding on tightly to his camera case—so tightly that his knuckles were white. It was a dead giveaway.

"I think the real diamond necklace is in Jean Alain's camera case, Ms. Darby," I said.

Ms. Darby marched across the room and grabbed the camera case from Jean Alain. "Give me that!" she cried out. She fumbled with the clasps for a moment, and the case clicked open.

"Try the lens case," I suggested.

Ms. Darby pried open the lens case—and a diamond necklace spilled out. The *real* diamond necklace.

"Mystery solved—again," Ms. Darby said with a sigh. "Elizabeth, call the police! Never mind, I'll do it myself. You and Jean Alain are going to jail for a long, long time. And it won't be a fake jail, either."

George's PDA started beeping as I walked into the wrap party that night. The party was on a boat on the Seine River. From inside I could hear voices, laughter, the clinking of glasses, and jazz music.

The tiny mailbox icon was flashing. For a second I held my breath, wondering if it was another message from DOOMSDAY246.

But it was just a message from George. It said:

```
I couldn't trace DOOMSDAY246's identity.
But I did find another e-mail address that
the person uses. It's LANPARTY2000. I hope
that helps. I'll keep trying. Love, G
```

I stared at George's message. LANPARTY2000.

For some reason, that name rang a bell. I closed my eyes and concentrated, trying to remember.

I felt a hand on my arm. I opened my eyes. It was Mary Lee. She was dressed in a pretty blue dress and matching high heels.

"Hey, Nancy," she said in a soft voice. "I wanted to, um, apologize."

"I've been worried about you, Mary Lee," I told her. "What's going on? Why have you been avoiding Hamish and me?"

Mary Lee sighed. "Now that the show is over, I can tell you," she said. "A couple of days ago, I got an e-mail on my personal whatchamacallit. My PDA. Like the thing you have. It said that I had to stay away from you and Hamish because the two of you were dangerous."

"Me . . . and Hamish? Dangerous?" I almost burst out laughing.

Mary Lee nodded. "That's what DOOMS-DAY246 said. Fish got the same e-mail. We didn't know what to do, so we just kind of took off and avoided everyone for a while."

I gasped. "DOOMSDAY246 e-mailed you and Fish, too?"

Mary Lee stared at me. "Yeah. Why? Did he e-mail *you*?"

"Sure did," I replied.

Out of the corner of my eye, I saw Chen and

Althea sitting together at a table, chowing down on hors d'oeuvres. Something clicked in my brain.

"Come on," I said to Mary Lee. "There's someone we need to talk to."

"Who?" Mary Lee asked me.

"DOOMSDAY246," I replied.

"Huh?" Mary Lee said, sounding surprised.

I led Mary Lee through the main room of the party boat. It had been decorated with balloons, streamers, and brightly colored banners that said things like CONGRATULATIONS, NANCY AND HAMISH! and SUPER DETECTIVES DREW AND WATSON! and FELICITATIONS!, French for "Congratulations!" A waiter rushed up to me and offered me a tray of canapés: tiny slices of bread adorned with smoked fish, vegetables, and cheeses. I took one and popped it into my mouth.

Mary Lee and I soon reached Chen and Althea's table. They glanced up at the same time. "Did you come over to rub it in, Drew?" Chen asked me with a sneer.

"Li, that's not a cool thing to say," Althea chided him.

I smiled at Chen. "Listen. I was just thinking about that T-shirt you were wearing on the first day. What did it say? LAN PARTY."

Chen frowned. "Yeah? What about it?"

"I guess you must like that phrase," I went on. "That's why you use it for an e-mail name, too. LANPARTY2000."

Chen turned pale. "How did you—"

"And your other e-mail name. DOOMSDAY246. Where did you come up with that one?" I persisted.

Chen gaped. He didn't say anything.

"You're DOOMSDAY246?" Mary Lee gasped. "You're the one who sent me and Fish those scary e-mails? About Nancy and Hamish being dangerous and all?"

Chen regarded her silently. Then he turned to me. "Look, I'm sorry," he said finally. "When I found out that I was going to be on *Mystery Solved!* I, uh, hacked into the show's database and found out who the other contestants were. I researched everyone and quickly deduced that you were going to be my number one competition."

"Me?" I said dumbly.

Chen nodded. "Yeah, you. I read all the newspaper articles about you. You may be an amateur detective, but you have a killer rep. I wanted to spook you, throw you off your game. I thought that if I sent you that message . . ." His voice trailed off. "When you didn't seem to be backing off the mystery, I sent that e-mail to Mary Lee and Fish, so they'd stop helping you. I was going to send one to Hamish, too. But then you guys solved the case."

He added, "Anyway, I apologize. It wasn't fair play. And I'm sorry for giving Tyler your e-mail address,

Nancy. He asked me if I could find it for him, and I gave it to him for, uh, some monetary compensation."

I smiled. Leave it to Tyler to pay for my e-mail address. "Apology accepted," I told Chen.

Mary Lee rolled her eyes. "Uh, I guess me, too," she said. "You need to apologize to Fish, too. What you did was not nice, Chen Li."

"I know, I know," Chen said sheepishly. "I'll never do it again. Okay?"

"So how's it feel to solve *two* mysteries?"

I turned around at the sound of the familiar male voice. It was Tyler. He, Wendy, and Fish were standing there. Tyler was wearing a tux. Wendy was wearing a killer black dress with silver sequins. Fish was wearing jeans and a Hawaiian-print shirt. Fish walked up to Mary Lee and put his arm around her.

Wendy raised her glass of sparkling cider. "Congratulations, Nancy. You and Hamish definitely deserved to win."

"Thanks," I said. "You all did a great job too."

"I've been wondering," Tyler said curiously. "How did you figure out that Jean Alain and Elizabeth were about to take off with the real necklace?"

"I didn't figure that out until the very end," I admitted. I explained about Jean Alain trying to sidetrack me with his revelation about a "mole" and offering me his "help" in other ways. I also explained about overhearing two people talking in the hallway outside my hotel room, and about the attempted break-in.

"Jean Alain and Elizabeth confessed everything to the police this afternoon," I went on. "They met on the job and somehow got to talking about how they wanted to make some serious money. They came up with a scheme to steal the diamond necklace. Plan A was for Elizabeth to discover the whereabouts of the necklace by keeping her eyes and ears open around Dee Darby. Plan B was for them to wait until one of the contestants found the necklace, then switch it for the fake during an unguarded moment." I added, "The security device was a complication too. They realized that either Ms. Darby or Mr. Laurier had to turn the device off before anyone could even *touch* the necklace—much less steal it."

"Wow, Plan B sounds superrisky," Wendy commented.

I nodded. "That's why they got caught. I think that they had *just* made the switch and hidden the necklace in Jean Alain's camera case when I walked into the library."

"Amazing," Tyler said, shaking his head.

"The irony was, Jean Alain and Elizabeth needed me—or one of you guys—to find the necklace so they could steal it," I said. "They picked me for some reason and decided to sneak me clues and stuff, to help me along. How bizarre is that?"

Fish grinned at me. "Nancy, you are wiser and deeper than the ocean itself. I am *definitely* writing a song in your honor when I get home to Hawaii."

Dee Darby got up on stage and clapped her hands. "Nancy Drew and Hamish Watson come on up onstage; it's time to receive your prize!"

Out of the corner of my eye, I saw Hamish strolling in my direction. He had added a festive-looking black silk scarf to his usual Sherlock Holmes outfit. He joined me at my side, and we walked across the room together. People began clapping and calling out our names. Cameramen swarmed around us. Flashbulbs popped. Gold and silver confetti rained down on our heads. . . .

George, Bess, Dad, Hannah, and I sat on the couch, munching the organic barbeque-flavored popcorn that Bess had brought over. Dee Darby's face filled the TV screen.

"It's time to raise our glasses to our winners, Nancy Drew and Hamish Watson!" she exclaimed.

I blinked at the TV set as Hamish and I appeared on screen. Even after watching the entire *Mystery Solved!* episode with my friends, Dad, and Hannah, it still felt weird to see myself on TV. There I was— three months ago, experiencing one of the most exciting moments of my life. Not only had I won the contest, I'd also solved a real mystery.

"So, Hamish? What are you going to do with your half of the prize money?" Dee Darby was asking Hamish on TV.

"I've always dreamed of commissioning a statue of Sherlock Holmes to put in front of my bookstore," Hamish replied.

"What about you, Nancy?" Ms. Darby asked me.

"I promised some people back home that I would donate it to River Heights Relief, to build a homeless shelter," I said. "A very generous lady named Mrs. Rackham is matching my donation. That means one hundred thousand dollars total for the shelter."

"Sherlock Holmes would have approved of such a good cause," Hamish piped up. Everyone laughed and clapped. More confetti rained down on our heads.

As the show cut to a commercial, George and Bess both slapped me high fives. "Nancy Drew, you are a star!" George cried out.

"And you looked the part," Bess added. "I'm so glad you followed my fashion advice and wore the black dress for the party."

Dad and Hannah both hugged me. "We're so proud of you," Dad said with a smile.

I hugged them back and wondered where my next mystery would take me. . . .

Turn the page for a sneak peek at the new

GIRL DETECTIVE®

NANCY DREW

AND THE

UNDERCOVER BROTHERS®

HARDY BOYS

Super Mystery

TERROR ON TOUR

CAROLYN KEENE
and
FRANKLIN W. DIXON

FRANK

A NEW MISSION

"Pop it in, already!" Joe said.

I glanced at him. He was jumping around like an overcaffeinated monkey. Then again, that could pretty well describe my brother most of the time. He isn't what you'd call patient.

"I'm working on it," I told him.

I couldn't resist slowing my movements a little just to bug him. First I slid the CD slooowly out from between the pages of the ad booklet. I took my time as I made a leisurely stroll across my bedroom toward the game console on my desk. My hand moved like molasses as I reached toward the power button. . . .

"Frank!" Joe exclaimed.

I grinned. Joe is way too easy to mess with sometimes.

But I didn't make him suffer any longer. I was just as eager as he was to see what our next mission would be. I slid the CD into the machine and hit Play.

"*Greetings, ATAC agents,*" said the familiar voice of Q., our boss at ATAC. "*Your next mission begins in six days, and involves out-of-state travel. Please press Continue if you would like to accept the mission. Your briefing will follow.*"

"No brainer." Joe lunged for the console and pressed the button.

I opened my mouth to remind him that we're supposed to be a team, and that it would be nice if he consulted me before pressing Continue. Or before climbing through a window in an abandoned house, for that matter.

But then I shut it again. Joe will never change. Besides, the message was starting.

A silvery flash filled the screen, and the ear-shattering scream of an electric guitar poured out of the speakers. I cast a nervous glance at the bedroom door, hoping Mom and Aunt Trudy were still safely downstairs.

When I looked at the screen again, it was filled with smoke. A dark figure strode out from the middle of it, carrying a microphone. He had shaggy dark hair and was wearing leather pants and a mask.

"*Hello ATAC agents!*" the mystery man on the screen shrieked into the microphone. "*Are you ready to rock? Because you're going to Rockapazooma!*"

"Whoa!" Joe exclaimed as the masked guy paused to

play a sizzling lick on his guitar. "Did you hear that? Rockapazooma!"

"Isn't that some big concert out in the Midwest?" I said. "I saw something about it on TV the other day."

Joe looked shocked. "It's not just *some* concert, dude," he said. "It's *the* concert!"

I shrugged. I like music as much as the next guy, but I'm not obsessed with it like Joe. He wears his DJ Razz T-shirt all the time. Aunt Trudy has forbidden him from wearing his Lethal Injection shirt, though. For some reason she thinks the picture of one band member holding up another band member's severed head is disgusting.

Onscreen, the guitar-playing guy was fading out. He was replaced by the image of crowds of people partying at an outdoor concert.

Q.'s voice continued the message in voice-over. *"Rockapazooma is more than just the biggest concert of the year. It's a way for musicians and sponsors to raise awareness of the environmental problems facing the world today: deforestation, endangered species, global warming, and other issues. All proceeds of the show will go to groups working to fight these problems. So not only will fans get to enjoy an entire day of great live music, but they'll be helping to save the world, too. Sounds like a win-win, right?"*

"Totally," Joe interjected with a grin. "Especially for us!"

"*However,*" the voice continued, "*ATAC and its affiliated agencies have intercepted buzz indicating that someone may intend to disrupt the concert. Unfortunately we can't tell you much more than that. The stakes are high, and if the wrong people were to intercept this message, it could endanger the mission—and your lives.*"

"Helpful," I commented.

Joe was grinning. "I can't believe we're really going to Rockapazooma!"

Way to stay on task, I thought. But I didn't say anything, because the voice-over was continuing.

"*Your identities for this mission are Jack and Jimmy Leyland, ordinary music fans. You will have to stay on the lookout for anything suspicious. We may try to mobilize another set of agents to work on this case as well, but you should proceed as if you are the only agents present. We are working closely with the local police department and FBI office on this case, so if you run into any serious trouble, please consider them your allies. A crowd-control tool is included in the CD case in case you run into any trouble. As usual this mission is top secret. Good luck, and rock on, ATACers. This CD will be reformatted in five seconds. Five, four, three, two, one . . .*"

I steeled myself for more screaming guitars when the disk switched to music. Instead, a female voice poured out of the speakers. The song was catchy, but I didn't recognize it.

"Who's this?" I asked.

Joe stared at me. "Man, you're even more out of touch than I thought. It's only the Royal We, the hottest new band in the known world."

"The Royal We?" It rang a bell. "Wait, isn't that the band with the young female singer—"

"Who's amazingly hot?" Joe finished for me. "Yeah, her name's Kijani."

"I was going to say, the young female singer who sought asylum here from her home country in Africa." I searched my mind for the details. I'd read a story on the singer a few weeks ago in a news magazine. "She's part of a royal family, I think. That's how they came up with the idea for the name of the band."

"Whatever." Joe shrugged.

"Joe, we're not going to Rockapazooma to look at girls," I reminded him.

Joe grinned. "The guy on the CD said to watch out for anything suspicious," he said. "I'll be keeping my eye out for suspiciously hot girls."

I suddenly remembered something. "Hey, didn't the CD say something was included with it?" I grabbed for the jewel case, which I'd dropped on the desk near the game console.

Joe looked over my shoulder as I examined it. "What is it?" he asked. "Must be pretty small."

"Here we go." I spotted two cylindrical silvery objects tucked into the casing. Each was about the size and shape of a pack of breath mints. Joe grabbed one and I picked up the other.

I turned it over in my hands. The only thing breaking the smooth silver surface was a tiny button at one end. "I wonder how they—"

"*YOW!*" Joe yelled, jumping about three feet in the air. He dropped his tool and shook his right hand violently, hopping up and down and grimacing. "That thing has a serious *bite* to it! Take my advice, Frank—don't touch the end and press the button at the same time."

That's my brother—the human guinea pig. "So they're like miniature cattle prods." I figured that could definitely come in handy in a crowd full of rowdy concert-goers.

"Boys?" Aunt Trudy's voice floated through the door. "Is everything okay in there? What's with all the yelling?"

"We're fine, Aunt Trudy," I called back. "Sorry about the noise."

As her footsteps faded away, I looked at Joe. "That reminds me. How're we going to explain this one?"

Keeping our ATAC work a secret from Mom and Aunt Trudy is always a challenge. Dad helps us cover when he can. But mostly Joe and I just need to be really good at coming up with stories to explain our comings and goings.

"Easy," Joe said. "We tell the truth—sort of."

I blinked. "Huh?"

Joe grinned. "We say we're going to Rockapazooma,"

he said. "Lethal Injection and DJ Razz are both playing the show. Everybody knows I'm into them. So we say I called in to a radio contest or something, and won an all-expenses-paid trip for two to the show."

I had to admit it was a great plan. "Keep it simple," I said, echoing one of Dad's favorite sayings. "Yeah, that could work." Then I realized what he'd said and grimaced. "Lethal Injection, huh?"

"Yeah! I can't wait to see them live," Joe exclaimed. "It's going to be awesome! I wonder what the death stunt will be? Oh! And I hope they play 'White Hot Death'—that song rocks."

I couldn't help grinning at his enthusiasm, even if I didn't share it. "Yeah," I said. "Remind me to pack my earplugs, okay?"

"Whoa!" Joe climbed out of the taxi. "Check it out. This place is packed already."

I finished paying the driver. Then I straightened up and looked around.

Joe was right. The concert venue was a seething mass of humanity. Now that we were there, there was no question about why we might need those crowd-control devices if we were to do any investigating. We weren't even inside and we could barely move.

We were standing near the parking area, which was bumper to grill with vehicles. A tall chain-link fence blocked off the enormous field where the concert would take place. Through it I could see a huge stage surrounded by an equally huge spiderweb of lights and rigging. Sixty-foot-tall speaker towers stood on either side of the stage. Giant video screens atop more speakers dotted the football-field-size area in front of it.

I could also see people. Lots of people.

"And here I thought we were arriving nice and early," I said. "The music doesn't even start for more than an hour!"

"Well, we're here now." Joe headed toward the nearest entry point. "Let's get inside."

We waited in line for our turn. A bored-looking security guard glanced at our passes, which we'd picked up from the pilot of the private plane that had flown us in from Bayport that morning.

"Welcome to Rockapazooma." The guard stifled a yawn. He was wearing a neon green T-shirt with the concert's logo—a smiling planet Earth playing an electric guitar. It was kind of dorky, but it got the point across. "Are you carrying any liquids, weapons, or electronic devices?"

"No way," Joe answered for both of us. We took out our cell phones and pocket change and put them in the guy's little tray.

"Step through the metal detector and enjoy the show."

I thought about the mini-electric-prod in my jeans pocket. What if the metal detector picked it up and we got kicked out?

But I should have known ATAC would be on top of things. We both made it through the metal detector without a buzz.

"Guess those little shocker doodads don't have much metal in them," Joe commented as we stepped away.

"Yeah." I stuck my cell back in my pocket and glanced around. From inside the gates the place looked even more crowded. "I guess we should still follow our original plan—walk around and try to get a feel for the place before it gets any busier."

"Are you sure?" Joe teased. "You mean, you don't have a backup plan?"

I didn't bother to answer. I was still feeling kind of uneasy about the whole situation. It was weird not knowing what this mission was about. There had been times when ATAC had been more vague with us than I would have liked, but this took the cake.

Still, that didn't mean we couldn't attack it logically. Right?

"Let's make a circuit of the whole place," I suggested. "We can scope out the best places to see the crowd."

"The crowd?" Joe glanced toward the stage. A bunch

of roadies were up there moving equipment around. "What about the bands?"

I started walking. "We're not here to watch the bands."

"We're supposed to keep an eye on *everything*," Joe pointed out. "That means the bands too."

"Whatever." I stopped and shaded my eyes against the sun. "Let's head for that speaker tower out in the middle first, and then—"

"Hey!" Joe grabbed my arm. "Check out the babe."

A young woman of about nineteen was doing some kind of solo interpretive dance nearby. Her eyes were closed, and her arms were waving over her head. She was dressed in nothing but a grass skirt and a skimpy bikini top that left very little to the imagination.

"We're not here for *that*, either," I told Joe. "Come on."

Joe shot one last glance at the teen. Then he jogged to catch up with me.

"You're not going to let me have any fun at all on this trip, are you?"

He was giving me the Look. I hate the Look. It makes me feel like I'm a hundred and one years older than Joe, instead of just one. It almost made me ashamed that I really *had* packed earplugs for this trip. They were in my jeans pocket right now, right next to the mini-cattle-prod. Good thing Joe didn't know that. Otherwise I'd probably be facing the Look times ten.

But I couldn't let it get to me. We had business to take care of. "Grow up, Joe," I told him. "We're here on a case, remember?"

"Yeah, I know," he said. "But that doesn't mean we can't have fun, too."

We were still moving through the crowd as we talked. At that moment we were off to the right side of the stage. Just ahead I noticed several security guards wearing those neon green planet shirts. They were standing in front of another chain-link fence. Behind it were a bunch of big gleaming charter-type buses and double-wide trailers.

Joe spotted them too. "That looks like the backstage area," he said. "Let's sneak in and take a look."

"Sneak in?" I glanced at the guards. Each of them alone easily weighed more than Joe and I did together. "I don't think so."

"Why not?" Joe said. "You're the one who's always saying we should be thorough, and—whoa! Check *her* out!"

Glancing where he was staring, I saw three girls about our own age. Unlike Ms. Bikini Dancer, they were all fully clothed in shorts and T-shirts. The slim girl with reddish-blond hair and the athletic-looking brunette were both cute. But their friend really stood out in the crowd. She was blond and curvy, with the kind of face that made you want to walk right up to her and say hi.

I realized I was staring. I also realized that Joe was already hurrying toward the girls.

Uh-oh. I took off after him.

"Hi," he was saying to the blond when I caught up. "I'm Joe. What's your—"

"Excuse us," I interrupted.

I grabbed his arm. He struggled a little, but I dragged him away.

The blond girl giggled and waved. Her dark-haired friend rolled her eyes.

"Dorks," she muttered.

The third girl, the one with the reddish hair, just watched us go. She looked amused.

"What's the big idea?" Joe finally broke free of my grip. He looked around for the girls, but they'd already been swallowed up in the crowd. "Those three looked suspicious. I was just going to question them a little."

"Yeah, right." I let out a snort. "Get your hormones under control, Mr. Slick. We've got work to do."

Joe snapped to attention and saluted. "Sir, yes sir!"

Just then there was a commotion up ahead. A camera crew was emerging from the backstage area. They were surrounding a gorgeous young woman holding a microphone. I recognized her as Annie Wu, a VJ from the music television station. Fans were pushing forward, trying to catch a better look at the VJ. As soon as the crew was through, the guards returned to their positions in front of the backstage gate.

"We really need to get in there," Joe said. "Let's see if we can find a weak spot in the fence."

At least he was back on track with the mission. "Okay," I said. "Can't hurt to check it out."

I still wasn't sure trying to sneak in was the best use of our time right then. But at least it would distract Joe from girls for a few minutes.

Less than ten minutes later we were in. It wasn't even a challenge to our ATAC skills—we just walked along the fence until we came to a spot where two sections of the fence came together. Or rather, where they *didn't* come together. They were hooked to each other with a chain, but there was a space between them just big enough for us to squeeze through. There was a green-shirted guard nearby, but he was talking on a cell phone with his back to us, so we got through easily.

Once we were inside, nobody paid any attention to us. There were tons of people running around, looking busy and important. We started walking, taking in the whole scene.

"Look," I said. "That must be the official press area."

There were a bunch of big portable lights set up around a small stage containing a couple of director's chairs with the Rockapazooma logo on them. A neon green screen stood behind the stage.

Joe glanced that way and nodded. "Guess nobody's getting interviewed right now," he said. "Come on, let's check out the band trailers."

We wandered deeper into the backstage area. Trailers, buses, and semis loomed all around us. There were fewer people walking around in this section, although there were big, muscular guys guarding some of the trailers and buses.

After turning a corner we passed a large but nondescript trailer. Just ahead I noticed a cotton-candy pink tour bus painted with airy white swirls.

"Wonder which band came in that thing?" I said.

"Bet it wasn't DJ Razz." Joe grinned. "If he was seen in a bus like that, his fans would disown him."

I laughed. "Yeah, but what better way to travel incognito?" I said. "Nobody would ever guess Razz was inside that Barbie-doll-looking thing."

"True." Joe glanced over at the generic-looking trailer we were passing at the moment. "But I still bet he'd rather—"

Joe was cut off by a sudden, bloodcurdling scream.

CHANCE ENCOUNTERS

Ned had to be at the concert early. Bess, George, and I weren't complaining about that. We were so psyched to be at Rockapazooma that we were all about to burst.

"I need to go sign in at the press tent," Ned told us after we cleared the metal detector at the entrance gate. "Want to come along? I can try to get you guys backstage with me."

"Awesome!" George's eyes sparkled. "Maybe we'll see Nick Needles or Mike Manslaughter walking around!"

"Mike Manslaughter?" Bess wrinkled her nose. "Let me guess—another member of Lethal Injection?"

"Duh. He's only the lead singer." George tugged on Ned's arm. "Come on, let's go!"

We wound our way through the crowd. I couldn't believe it was already so packed. The show wouldn't start for almost ninety minutes, but it looked as if at least half of the expected 200,000 people were already there. Some people had set up folding chairs in front of the stage, while others were lying out in the sun on picnic blankets or tossing Frisbees or playing Hacky Sack. There were long lines at the refreshment stands and the souvenir booths, and even longer ones at the restrooms.

"Wow," I said. "This is wild! I can't believe we're really here."

Ned reached over and squeezed my hand. "Having fun so far?"

"Definitely." I smiled and squeezed back. "I just can't believe how crowded it is. Good thing we brought cell phones in case we get separated. Because there's no way you could ever find someone in this . . ."

My voice trailed off as I spotted the backstage gate, which was just a few yards ahead now. Was I seeing things?

"What's wrong?" Ned asked.

Bess blinked. "Is that Deirdre?" she exclaimed.

There was no mistaking it. A line of security guards dressed in neon green shirts with the concert logo on them were standing in front of the gate. Deirdre was glaring up at one of them, a man approximately the same size and shape as a refrigerator. He stared at her impassively, his meaty arms crossed over his chest. I guessed that his green T-shirt had to be a size XXXL.

"Oh, man," George muttered, staring at Deirdre in disbelief. "We've been here twenty minutes, and look who we run into. What are the odds?"

I shook my head. "I don't know. But it looks like maybe that backstage pass of hers isn't working too well."

We hurried forward. Deirdre was waving her hands around and whining at the huge guard. Now that we were closer, I could see that the name tag pinned to the guard's shirt identified him as TYREESE—SECURITY.

". . . and if you had more than two brain cells to rub together, you'd realize that I'm obviously telling the truth," Deirdre was complaining as we got close enough to overhear. "I was told quite clearly that this ticket gives me free admission to the *entire* concert grounds. And that obviously means I should be able to go backstage without some oversized rent-a-guard stopping me, and . . ."

As we all listened in, George's expression changed from annoyance to delight. Finally she stepped forward.

"Well, hello, DeeDee," she said. "Having some problems, are we?"

Deirdre spun around, looking startled. "Oh, it's you," she spat. "Mind your own business. I'm just trying to explain to this doofus that I need to get backstage." She spun around to glare at the guard again. "Just wait until my friends Kijani and Nicky Needles hear about this. Oh, and Toni Lovely, too. They're all close friends of mine, you know. Did you hear me? Once my good friend Kijani hears about this, you'll never work security in this town again!"

The guard didn't look impressed by her threat. "Nobody gets backstage without the proper authorization," he rumbled in a deep voice. "Not without going through me first."

Ned shot me an amused glance. "Maybe this isn't the best time to try to get you guys backstage after all," he murmured.

George heard the guard too. She looked disappointed, but she nodded. "We'll have to meet up with you later."

"Definitely." Ned patted the cell phone clipped to his belt. "See you."

He stepped past Deirdre, who was still ranting at the top of her lungs. Approaching one of the other guards, Ned held up his press pass. The guard peered at it, then waved him through.

"See you, Ned!" George sang out loudly, waving at him. "Have fun backstage!"

Deirdre heard and shot her a dirty look. George smiled pleasantly in return. "You too, Deirdre," she said sweetly. "*If* you ever get back there, that is."

Bess grabbed her by the arm and dragged her away.

"Come on," she chided with a smile. "Stop teasing Deirdre. It's not nice."

"Says who?" George grinned.

Just then I noticed a guy around our age charging toward us. He was cute, with wavy blond hair and blue eyes. "Who's that?" I asked my friends. "Someone you know?"

Bess and George both shook their heads. "Looks like he wants to know us, though," George commented. "*One* of us, anyway."

As he got closer, it became obvious that the blond guy was staring at Bess. That was nothing new. With her blond hair, great figure, and dimples, Bess turns heads wherever she goes. Guys are always coming up to her on the street, in restaurants, at the mall, in the post office—pretty much anywhere. Luckily Bess never lets all the attention go to her head. In fact, she kind of hates it.

The guy skidded to a stop in front of us. "Hi," he said breathlessly, his eyes locked on to Bess. "I'm Joe. What's your—"

"Excuse us."

Another guy had suddenly appeared. He was a little taller and leaner than the blond guy, but just as good-looking, with dark hair and an intense expression on his angular face. Without another word, he grabbed the first guy's arm and yanked him away.

Bess giggled and waved as the two guys moved away.

"Dorks," George muttered, rolling her eyes.

I just watched in amusement as the blond guy struggled against his friend's grip. "Too bad, Bess," I commented as the two guys were lost behind a group of teenagers batting around a beach ball. "Those guys were pretty cute."

Just then Deirdre's voice floated toward us from back by the gate. "Fine!" she shrieked. "You win, okay? But this isn't the last you've seen of me! As soon as I get in touch with Kijani and Nick, I'll be back!"

I glanced over that way just in time to see Deirdre storm off, her face frozen in a furious scowl. She pushed between a couple of the beach-ball-tossing teens.

"Yo!" one of them said in surprise. "Watch it!"

"Watch it yourself," Deirdre snarled, not slowing her pace as she stalked off into the crowd.

"Come on." George was already heading off after her. "If her head's about to explode, I want to be there to see it."

I had to admit I was at least mildly curious about what Deirdre would do next. As I've already mentioned, she isn't the type to give up easily on something she wants.

"Okay, why not," I said. "We still have a while until the concert starts."

"Oh, Nancy." Bess sounded amused. "You'll do anything to pretend you have a mystery to solve."

I shrugged and grinned. "You're right," I told Bess with a smile. "It's the mystery of how Deirdre Shannon is going to enjoy herself at this concert if she can't get backstage to rub elbows with the stars."

George gestured to us impatiently. "Hurry up—we're losing her!"

Even in the ever-growing crowd it wasn't too difficult to keep track of Deirdre. All we had to do was follow the chorus of *Hey*s and *Watch it*s and *Ow*s she left in her wake as she rudely pushed past people. It also helped that she was wearing a hot pink shirt with yellow trim. Deirdre likes to stand out.

We stayed back a few yards, trying not to let her see us while keeping her in sight. As we walked, we also had a chance to look around and to see more of the concert area.

Deirdre's path was leading us deeper into the crowd in front of the stage, which had grown thicker as the concert's start time drew closer. People were sitting, standing, dancing, or wandering across the field. Here and there we could see the bright green of a security guard's T-shirt among them. Up on the stage, workers were setting up microphones and busily moving equipment back and forth. The atmosphere, which had been relaxed when we arrived, was sizzling with anticipation.

"Hey, look!" Bess said, pointing as one of the video screens hanging over the huge stage flickered to life. It showed the Rockapazooma logo for a moment or two, then started flashing images of trees, wildlife, oceans, and other scenes of nature.

"Almost time!" George had to raise her voice to be heard over the buzz of conversation, laughter, and random outbursts of singing all around us.

I glanced ahead, catching a glimpse of Deirdre's pink shirt. She had just passed the nearest large speaker tower, which was located in the middle of the front section of the audience area about fifty yards from the stage. Judging by the direction she was going, I guessed she was heading for the line of refreshment stands off to the left side of the stage area.

"Maybe we should start looking for a spot to watch from," Bess suggested. "It looks like we're losing Deirdre anyway."

Turning to glance once more toward the speaker tower, I saw that she was right. Deirdre had disappeared behind a cluster of middle-aged men who were tossing around a football.

"Okay," I said. "Where do you want to go?"

Bess opened her mouth, but her answer was drowned out as the speakers suddenly crackled to life. There was a burst of music, then a voice: "Testing, testing—earth, air, sea . . ."

The crowd reacted immediately, letting out an excited roar. All around us, people surged forward, everyone trying to get closer to the stage.

Bess grabbed my hand. "Come on!" she yelled. "Let's go this way!"

I nodded and started to follow. But something made me glance over toward that speaker tower again—the last place I'd seen Deirdre. At that moment several of the middle-aged men tackled one of their friends, and I could see past them to the base of the metal tower.

There was a flash of hot pink. Deirdre?

"Come on, Nancy!" George shouted in my ear, giving me a shove.

"Wait!" I said, though I doubted anyone could hear me—the speakers had just emitted another ear-shattering burst of music.

But I yanked free of Bess's hand, straining to see through the crowd. There it was again—the flash of pink.

I gasped. It *was* Deirdre . . . and she was shrieking and struggling as an enormous man in a green security T-shirt roughly dragged her off.

HARDY BOYS

UNDERCOVER BROTHERS™

They've got motorcycles,
their cases are ripped from the headlines,
and they work for ATAC:
American Teens Against Crime.

CRIMINALS, BEWARE:
THE HARDY BOYS ARE
ON YOUR TRAIL!

Frank and Joe tell all-new stories of crime,

danger, death-defying stunts, mystery, and teamwork.

Ready? Set? Fire it up!

She's sharp.

She's smart.

She's confident.

She's unstoppable.

And she's on your trail.

MEET THE NEW NANCY DREW

Still sleuthing,

still solving crimes,

ut she's got some new tricks up her sleeve!

NANCY DREW

girl detective™